"I'd like to hire you for another job."

Penn explained in a machine-gun burst of words, "I want that boy. My only hope is to walk into that court with a capable, happy wife on my arm. I need somebody who can accept the temporary nature of the whole affair, and that's why I want you, Philomena."

Phil took a deep breath. "You want me to—"

"Marry me. There will be proper compensation for it all, Philomena," he said. "Well?"

"I'm thinking," she blurted out angrily. "Surely you don't expect a girl to hear something like that and promptly fall at your feet in rapture?"

After he'd gone, Phil sat for more than an hour thinking. But when she thought about her reaction to *him*, her mind shied away from the subject like a nervous mare!

EMMA GOLDRICK describes herself as a grandmother first and an author second. She was born and raised in Puerto Rico, where she met her husband, a career military man from Massachusetts. His postings took them all over the world, which often led to mishaps—such as the Christmas they arrived in Germany before their furniture. Emma uses the places she's been as backgrounds for her books, but just in case she runs short of settings, this prolific author and her husband are always making new travel plans.

Books by Emma Goldrick

EMMA GOLDRICK

if love be blind

Harlequin Books

TORONTO • NEW YORK • LONDON
AMSTERDAM • PARIS • SYDNEY • HAMBURG
STOCKHOLM • ATHENS • TOKYO • MILAN

Harlequin Presents first edition December 1987
Second printing November 1987
ISBN 0-373-11035-9

Original hardcover edition published in 1987
by Mills & Boon Limited

CHAPTER ONE

PHILOMENA helped the two little girls into their coats and hurried them to the door. The bride and groom had left an hour ago. Little Sally, barely eighteen, going off bravely, her heart in the hands of the boy next door. Samantha, twenty, and her doctor-husband, Albert had been called away long since. Deborah, twenty-one, was waiting on the porch for her two little twins, while husband John brought the car around. The rest of the guests had filtered away into the late afternoon sunshine. That leaves one little Indian, Phil told herself as she leaned tiredly against the door-jamb and waved.

Stillness settled over the house like a shroud. It had never been this quiet before. Never. She smiled at her daydreams, seldom allowed. Miss Practical Pill, the younger girls had often said of her. That was before they could form the 'ph' sound, of course. Later too, when they were feeling just a little bit saucy. Phil smiled at the reminiscence. She brushed her shoulder-length straw-coloured curls away from her neck and walked slowly back into the house.

There was a musty smell about everything. The living-room was crowded with dirty dishes and glasses. The kitchen was awash with clutter. Neither of her younger sisters had thought to stay and help with the clearing-up. They had been conditioned by years of, 'Oh, Phil will do that'. And so she would. But not just yet.

She wandered back into the living-room, fingering the

furniture as she went, feeling the metes and bounds of her world with tactile hands. The old armchair sagged to one side, but it was comfortable. She sank into it, and the stillness surrounded her again. *They were all married.* She relaxed against the back of the chair, and the load placed on her shoulders by her mother on her deathbed slipped away. Phil had been seventeen that year. 'Take care of the girls, Phil.' And with that faint whisper her mother had gone.

The wind rattled at a loose shutter. It seemed as if the house were trying to defy her. 'Mother,' she called as loudly as she could, 'have I done well?' Her voice echoed up the old staircase, bounced off the empty upstairs hall, and returned without answer. She hadn't expected any. Philomena Peabody shrugged her shoulders and went to face the cleaning.

She was up at her habitual hour of six the next morning, and it was not until she fumbled her way downstairs that she remembered. There was no school lunch to be made. No early breakfast for the three of them. No laundry to sort and start. Nothing. Her pattern of life had come unstuck. She went out into the warmth slowly. It was mid-February, and the fog clung to the valley as usual. Fog and low clouds were forecast in the local newspaper, the *Sacramento Bee*. Light northerly winds. High in the 50s, low in the 30s. High for the Sacramento River, 5.3 feet at I Street Bridge.

Her elderly Subaru stood bravely beside the house, in the shadow of a few scrawny old olive and almond trees. It was a family joke of sorts. Her grandfather had farmed one hundered and sixty acres. Now it was all reduced to the old house and a half-acre of regrets. Urban sprawl had conquered the rest. Sacramento was expanding beyond its boundaries, and here in Rancho Cordova the future of farming was written plain on the wall.

Phil shook her head. The regrets were all hers. She would have given anything to keep the farm—but bringing up three sisters was expensive, and her talents never had leaned towards farming. She shrugged her shoulders and put it behind her. The treasured old vehicle started at the first touch. She drove slowly over to Folsom Road, and then on to Route Fifty for the long commute. 'Maybe I could get a flat in town,' she mused as she wheeled through the typical California traffic jam. 'Maybe.'

She was still pondering when she came to the turn-off, jockeyed her way over to Fifteenth Street, and made it safely up to P Street. The small modern building that housed Pacific Mines and Metals was just a couple of blocks south of the golden dome of the State capitol building, and parking was always a problem. Which explained why she arrived at her office an hour late to find that the world of work had come unstuck also!

Betty Pervis, young, moderately attractive, and a newcomer to the typing pool, was standing by Phil's supervisory desk, shaking. All the other eight girls in the office were bent over their word-processors, but the tag-ends of wild conversation hung in the air. Phil put an arm around the young girl's shoulders, and laughed wryly at herself as she did so. Here I am, the Spinster Aunt, she thought. Twenty-seven years old, and over the hill!

'I'm never going back up there again,' Betty whimpered. 'Never!'

'Of course not,' Phil encouraged. 'Where?'

'His office,' she hiccupped. 'Mr Wilderman. Never!'

'Of course not. Here, use my chair. Harriet, could you

bring Betty a cup of coffee?' Phil bustled aimlessly,
knowing that the weeping woman needed time. When
the paper coffee-cup arrived she pressed it into the
twisting hands.

'Mr Wilderman isn't usually an—an ogre, Betty. He's
too old for that. Was he ill, or something?'

'Ill? Foul-mouthed, abusive—and I don't know why
you say old. He's——'

The internal telephone rang. Harriet answered it,
blushed, and set it down. 'He says—he wants somebody
else,' she reported grimly. 'And he's—wow.'

Phil patted Betty's shoulder and looked around the
room for volunteers. Every head ducked. 'So all right,'
she sighed. 'I'll go myself.' She nodded to Harriet,
gesturing in Betty's direction, then picked up a notebook
and a handful of pencils. It had been some months since
she had taken direct dictation. Just to be on the safe side
she reached into her desk drawer for her micro-recorder,
and slipped it into the upper pocket of her blazer.

The lift was the only fast-moving thing in the building.
It chuckled to a stop on the ninth floor and seemed to spit
her out on to the gold carpet. Which reinforced one of
Phil's long-held beliefs. *Anybody who was not an engineer
rated as nothing in this business, and even the lift knew it!*

It was quiet up here. Even the air-conditioning
equipment only dared to whisper. Six widely spaced
office doors, all closed, glared at her. 'You can't
intimidate me,' she murmured at them as she went down
the corridor. An adjacent door opened and two men
came out. They stared at her as if they had heard.

The door at the end of the corridor was half open. Phil
smoothed down her navy skirt, checked the recorder in
the pocket of her jacket, and pushed into the room. She

knew the outer office, having visited with Mrs Simmons a time or two, and once had actually substituted for the regular secretary for a couple of days.

The outer office was empty. Mrs Simmons favoured an electronic typewriter. It stood mute, covered, and her desk was bare. So Mrs Simmons was out today. Phil shrugged her shoulders. One piece of the puzzle had just fallen in place. Now, to beard the lion. She moved resolutely forward, taking deep breaths, building confidence. She rubbed the perspiration off her hand before she turned the door knob to the inner office.

The room was dim, with curtains pulled across the four wide windows. A man was slumped in the swivel chair behind the highly polished desk, with his back to her. She took two or three hesitant steps across the thick-pile rug, and stopped. The man, whoever he was, was not Mr Roger Wilderman. *That* worthy was sixty-five, bald on top, slightly rotund. The present occupant of the executive chair sported a full head of raven-black hair. The rest of him was huddled out of sight in the gloom. Phil cleared her throat as loudly as she could manage.

'Well, it's about time.' A deep voice, vibrating off the beige walls. A voice that brooked no arguments. 'Lost your tongue? Dear God, what do we hire these days, a bunch of rabbits? Sit down.'

Bully, Phil commented under her breath. Just the sort of man who required a little trimming. She settled herself into the chair beside his desk. He must have heard the rustle of her skirts, but he did not turn around.

'Letter to McPherson,' he began, and the words flowed. Phil had ten years of practice behind her pencil-point. It skated across the paper just a trifle ahead of his comments, pausing on occasion to let him catch up.

Three letters in a row, right off the top of his head. She acknowledged the expertise with a wry grin. With his back turned it was hard to see what notes he was using. He stopped. 'You've got all that?' The tone doubted it.

'Yes,' she said quietly. His chair half-turned, as if he could not believe it, and then returned to its former position.

'A memorandum to the entire staff,' he began. This time he spoke sharply, moving along faster. And at the end of each of the following memoranda, he increased his speed. Phil smiled again, grimly this time. He was waging war, and she had no intention of losing the battle. He stopped to organise his thoughts. Phil tucked her pencils neatly into her pocket, turned on the tape recorder, and settled back. After another ten minutes of racing, he stopped. 'You've got all that?'

'Yes,' she acknowledged. This time the chair turned around all the way, and he sat up out of his slouch.

'You're sure you have all that?'

'Positive.'

'Read me back that last paragraph.'

There was a moment to look him over. There was nothing in him of the Mr Wilderman she knew. Husky, in his early thirties, she thought. A mass of black hair that kept falling down over his right eye. A stern sort of face, that would have been more at home in a Western movie than in a boardroom. And wearing dark glasses!

'Well?' She snapped back to attention. One finger fumbled for the replay button on the recorder in her pocket, and his words rolled off the tape effortlessly. His head came up as he listened, and a smile played at the corners of his mouth. 'Smart,' he commented as the tape came to a hissing end. 'I don't know you, miss?'

'Peabody.' She gave it the New England pronunciation of her ancestors—Pee-buddy. It drew a chuckle.

'Miss Peabody,' he mused. 'You're a long way from New England. An immigrant?'

'Isn't everyone in California?' She was using her most prim voice, a soft contralto. He nodded as if acknowledging the comment.

'And what do you do for me, Miss Peabody?'

'I'm the supervisor of the typing pool,' she returned. 'But I don't do it for you. I do it for Mr Wilderman. I don't know who you are.'

'And that bothers you?'

'Among other things.' The words snapped out as if she were biting their tails off.

'Do I detect a little censure there?' His laughter was a low rumble. Pleasant, but also threatening. Philomena squared her shoulders and plunged into battle almost happily.

'You certainly do hear censure,' she snapped. 'I don't allow anyone in this corporation to yell and curse and storm at my girls!'

'Ah!' That chuckle again. 'Protecting your little lambs, are you, Miss—Peabody?'

'Very definitely,' she returned primly. 'Betty Pervis is downstairs crying. I'll have to send her home. We have a large workload. Failures of this kind by the executive staff cost the corporation money. It's something that's just not done, Mr—whoever you are. In addition, our union contract prohibits this sort of thing, Betty could file a grievance.'

'Ah!' It was almost as if he were licking his lips, relishing the fight to come. 'I do believe you're threatening me, Miss—Peabody. What the devil is your first name? I can't spend all day calling you Miss Peabody.'

'I—I don't think you really want to know,' she murmured.

'That bad, is it? Well, Peabody, I don't take well to threats, Maybe you should have your shop steward contact me.'

'Maybe I should,' she returned bluntly. 'Here I am.'

'Here you am what?' Was there a little laughter behind the words? Phil strained to think, to measure.

'Here I am, the shop steward,' she announced. 'I represent all the clerical and staff employees of this headquarters.'

'And?'

'And I think you owe Betty—Miss Pervis—an apology.'

'Or else? Lay it on the line, lady. I can hear the "or else" hanging in the air.'

'All right, if that's what you want to hear.' She squirmed in her chair. One does not throw lightning bolts casually, but having been cast they must be followed up. 'Ninety per cent of the people in this building are union members,' she said very coldly. 'It's conceivable that the union could strike over an issue like this. We had a strike three years ago, and——'

He waved it all aside with a casual hand. 'I've heard,' he said. 'Man, have I heard. So OK, lady——' He fumbled across the desk searching for something. 'Where the hell is that telephone——' Phil slid the internal telephone over beneath his hand. He grunted an acknowledgement. 'What's the number in your lion's den?'

'Lioness,' she muttered as she dialled the number and

handed the telephone back to him.

His gruff character disappeared the moment he started talking on the telephone. Warmth and charm flowed down the wires. Apologies were offered, spirits were soothed, and he hung up. 'There,' he groused. 'I hope that satisfies?'

'Yes,' she acknowledged grimly.

'That's all—just yes?'

'Yes.'

'You are without a doubt the least talkative woman I've met in ten years or more,' he returned. 'My grandmother was like that. To the point. I like that.'

Well, I don't particularly like you, she told herself. And restraining comments were pure torture. Luckily her ten years as a substitute mother had taught her to guard her tongue. She cleared her throat again. 'Will that be all, Mr——?'

The question hung in the air between them until he laughed again. 'I wish I could see what you look like,' he pondered. 'This damn eye problem—well. For your information, Peabody, my name *is* Wilderman. Penn Wilderman. I suppose you know my father?'

'I——' He had caught her off guard, almost to the point where her real personality was showing. She struggled to suppress it. 'I don't really know him,' she said, truthful to the detail. 'I did substitute for Mrs Simmons twice in the past five years, but I don't really know him. I'm not an executive, or anything like that.'

'So you'll have a chance to know me,' he snapped. 'My father has been overworking. My mother laid down the law to him last Friday. They've gone on a three-month cruise. So I flew home to take charge.'

'I'm sorry to hear that.'

'Sorry that I flew home?'

'No,' she snarled, 'don't twist my words. I'm sorry that your father isn't well. He is well liked.'

'Now what do you know?' he chuckled. 'A kind word from the guardian dragon. You must be years older than those light-brains I've seen. What do they call you down at the typing pool? Battleaxe?'

'Something like that,' she admitted. 'What's the trouble with your eyes?' she offered as a tangential thought.

'Snow blindness,' he returned. For a moment she was afraid he would refuse the bait, but he relaxed again and settled back into the deep swivel chair. 'I was doing some advisory work down at Little America, the South Polar station. We were caught in a blizzard, and a stupid female technician lost her protective glasses. I gave her mine—and before we could make it back to the base camp I got burned for it.' He fiddled at the frame of the dark glasses over his eyes, and then removed them. Both eyes were covered by small medical pads, taped in place across the bridge of his nose.

Phil would normally have reacted with sympathy. One thing held her back. That phrase, stupid *female* technician. With the emphasis on *female*. As if, had the technician been male, no catastrophe could possibly have occurred. She offered a non-committal 'Oh'.

'Don't be too enthusiastic,' he grated, replacing the glasses. 'It's not permanent. Three or four weeks more, perhaps, and then maybe I can figure out the horrible mess the corporation is in. How soon will you have that material ready?'

Phil looked down at her notes and considered. 'Perhaps two or three hours,' she offered.

'Perhaps? Is that the best you can do?'

'Yes,' she snapped. He leaned forward over the desk as if he were about to argue—or demand—or order. And then he thought better of it.

There's something funny going on here, Philomena told herself. Not with or about him, but with me. Why do I have this crazy itch when I look at him. He's a strange sort of executive, but I've seen stranger. What's wrong? Her logical mind could find no answer. She stood up, brushed down her clinging skirt, and started for the door.

'Peabody,' he called. She froze, with one hand already on the door knob. 'Come back here.' This wasn't his real voice. It was the smooth charmer of the telephone call. It doesn't really affect me, she told herself quickly. I'm not little Betty Pervis, to be soothed by a telephone call. But her feet carried her back to the side of the desk. She stood there, silently.

'Peabody?'

'Yes?'

'I couldn't even hear you breathe!' Which is not surprising, Phil told herself. I haven't been breathing since he called me back! The imprisoned air boiled out of her in a long deep sigh.

'Peabody. Ever done any nursing work?'

'Me? Of course not.'

'Funny. You sound like somebody's mother——'

'Oh, that sort of thing? Band-aids and Solarcaine? I've brought up three——'

'Just what I meant,' he chuckled. 'I need some drops in my eyes. Would you?' He gestured towards the side table. Phil walked over without thinking. Eyedrops and a syringe, all neat and tidy. 'Three of them?' he queried. 'Must have been quite a family.'

'Yes, it was,' she returned wryly. 'But they've all grown up, and the last one was married off just yesterday.' She picked up the syringe and came back. 'Lean back in the chair,' she ordered. He took off the glasses and settled back. She picked at the edge of the tape, and managed to free it. Black eyes, almost as black and deep as his hair. She hesitated. The past few minutes of conversation were whistling around in her head.

'Well,' he complained gruffly. 'I don't want major surgery.'

'No,' she returned. *What do they call you—battleaxe?* He must think I'm fifty years old—an old hag who cracks the whip down in the cellar of the building. Well, it serves him right! The drops cascaded out of the syringe. One or two lucky ones hit his eye. The others ran down his neck.

'Hey, I didn't ask for a bath,' he roared.

'It's all right,' she soothed, in the same tone she had used time after time with the girls. It worked. He settled back as she tidied up the mess with a tissue. 'And now the other one. Don't blink like that. I can't get the drops in while you flutter your eyelashes.' Long lashes, she noted. Curling up at the ends. I'd give my right arm for real lashes like that! Three precise drops flooded his other eye. He spluttered, blinked and reached up a hand. She stopped it in mid-flight.

'None of that,' she ordered. The hand stopped. She dabbed at the excess forced out on to his cheek, then carefully replaced the pads and the tape from the fresh supply on the table. 'There now.'

'That's a good boy,' he chuckled as he sat up. 'You forgot that part. You could be my mother, the way you talk.'

'I doubt that very much,' she sighed. 'And you can't see a thing?'

'Shapes. Light and dark. Movements,' he said. 'It's nothing permanent. So you wouldn't want to be my mother?'

'I should hope not.' It was hard to keep the disapproval out of her tone. And I really don't have any reason for disapproving, she reminded herself. He acted like a boor and a bully, and he apologised very nicely for it all. So either he's the world's biggest fake, or he's been raised with the nicest manners, or—lord, I don't know, do I?

'Thank you,' he offered. She jumped. While she had been debating, he had left his chair and was standing directly in front of her. He was not a huge man. Slender, whippet-like, and about a head taller than herself. Which isn't any great height, she told herself. But tall enough for me. If he hugged me, the top of my head would fit just under his chin! It was a fine supposition, but she was more than startled when he proceeded to demonstrate how true it was.

'What are you doing?' she snapped. It wasn't a gut reaction. She had some experience with hugging. From time to time over the past ten years she had found time to date a man—and to fight off a hug or two. Three times, to be exact. Raising three girls took a great deal of effort!

'I can't see you,' he grumbled, 'and I need to know something about you. I have to do it in Braille.'

'That's a good excuse.'

'I'm glad you think so.' He hadn't noticed her sarcasm, evidently. 'But I do wish you'd stand still. I can do this all by myself. You needn't wiggle against me.'

'I wasn't wiggling *against* you,' she stormed. 'I was wiggling—stop that!'

His hands had wandered through her hair, surrounded
her pert round face, touched on eyes, nose and mouth,
and were now diving over her chin and off into space.
They landed on the tops of her well rounded breasts,
paused for a second, and then trailed down her sides,
over her swelling hips, and——'

It had taken her that long to recover from the surprise
of it all. From the surprise, and from the shock of wild-
running senses which his touch had evoked. Her hand
moved automatically, bouncing off his cheek with a
satisfying thud, driving him back a step or two.

'Hey,' he protested.

'Hey is right, Mr Wilderman,' she stormed. 'I don't
allow people to take liberties with my—with me. I don't
see any reason why you should want to get to know me
better, because I doubt if I will be seeing you any time in
the near future. Mrs Simmons——'

'Mrs Simmons will be out for the day,' he returned.
'For a sweet little old lady you've got some marvellous
figure.'

'And a strong arm,' she threatened. 'And I never said
anything about being a sweeet little old lady.'

'No, you never did,' he chuckled. 'I'll strike out the
sweet, if you object. Why don't you run along to your little
cell and get that work out?'

'Yes,' she snapped, happy that he couldn't see the rose
hue that coloured her face. Blushes she had never learned
to suppress. She started for the door.

'You even walk softly,' he called after her. I'm darned
if I'll take that at face value, she told herself. The man
had a tongue that's hinged in the middle. One side sweet,
the other sour. She reached for the knob.

The door was one that swung inward. Just as her hand

moved forward the door swung open, catching her in the stomach. She staggered back a step, lost her balance, and sat down on the floor with a thump. 'This makes my day,' she groaned.

'Now what?' he asked. She turned to look at him. He had left the security of the desk and was fumbling his way across the room.

'Don't do that,' she called.

And behind her, at the door, a young voice. 'Don't do that, Dad!'

'Robert? What the devil are you doing here at this hour? And what happened to Peabody?'

Phil turned around. A boy stood in the door. A teenager, from the look of him. Painfully thin, blond hair neatly combed, wearing a suit and tie. A thin face. You could almost count the bones. Dad? He was a carbon copy of the man, in every way.

'Robert?'

'I—I think I knocked your—your lady over. She's sitting on the floor.'

'Well, help her up—or—come over here and lead me to her! Hurry up. She has fragile bones!'

Oh, do I? Phil ran a hand up and down her 'fragile bones'. Everything seemed to be in order, but her bottom gave notice of bruising to be reported later. The boy sidled around her as if she were a poised rattlesnake, and hurried to his father. The pair of them came over to her. 'Give me your hands, Peabody,' the father commanded.

She reached up hesitantly. 'I can get up for myself,' she said quietly.

'I'm sure you can,' Wilderman returned. 'Hands!'

She offered them both, smiling as they were swallowed into his. He might not be a big man, she thought, but his hands are for giants. How would you like them to——

He interrupted her wandering mind by moving around in front of her. The boy was doing his best to fade into the background. 'Put your foot up against mine,' he ordered. It hardly seemed worth a protest. She complied. 'Now, upsy-daisy.' His hands tightened on hers and up she went, as effortlessly as if he had been handling a five-pound parcel. 'There now. OK?'

Those darned hands again, sweeping up and down her body, brushing at her skirt, touching her in places where they had no right to be. She slapped at the hands, and he withdrew them.

'That's better than the last time.' He was so close that his whisper echoed in her ear.

'Don't press your luck,' she retorted. But his hands dropped to her shoulders, and before she could duck out of the way he planted a light kiss on her forehead. 'Don't *do* that,' she muttered through clenched teeth.

'Robert?' He turned Phil around in the approximate direction of the boy, who moved a step or two closer.

'Robert, I want you to meet Miss Peabody. She's the nice lady who has been helping me out.'

'She looks like——' the boy started to say. His father silenced him with an upraised hand.

'Don't say it,' he was admonished. 'She's a lovely lady. Shake hands.'

Phil worked up a smile, and offered her hand. The boy moved away and clasped both hands behind his back. Like that, huh, Phil thought. Shake hands and come out fighting? Well, have I got a surprise for you, sonny. I don't give a darn!

'I want you two to be friends,' his father said, evidently thinking the handshake had been effected.

'Yes, I can see that,' Phil retorted. 'And now if you *gentlemen* will excuse me, I have work to do.'

His ear caught the sarcasm this time. He looked down at her, puzzlement written all over his face. She shrugged herself loose from his hands, picked up her scattered pads and equipment, and rushed out of the door, leaving it open behind her.

'But, Dad, she looks like——' The boy was trying it again as she whizzed down the corridor. All of a sudden, the upper reaches of the Pacific Mine and Metal Corporation had taken on a threatening atmosphere. She dived for the protection of her own little empire on the ground floor.

CHAPTER TWO

BY the time the weekend rolled around, Phil was happy
to stay at home. Her trip to the executive suite had not
been repeated, but images had hung in her mind. Strange
images, that caused her more than one dreaming
moment when she should have been working. His face,
bad manners and all. His eyes, that pulled at her pity, his
hands that stabbed at her raw emotions and left her
wriggling on her chair. The boy. Thirteen going on fifty-
five. Rigid speech, formal airs, and an unhappy shadow
trying to hide behind his eyes. A strange pair.

To keep them out of her hair on Saturday she house-
cleaned. Polished, scrubbed, dusted, until the old house
sparkled. There was nothing to be done outside. Even in
California, February spells winter, and many a night the
temperature would be down to thirty degrees, just below
the frost line. So she had bedded all her flowers in early
December, burying them under a load of seaweed
imported up the Sacramento River from the ocean,
ninety-five miles away.

A walk through the remains of her orchard helped a
little. There were branches on the ground from the
ancient olive trees and the equally ancient walnut trees.
The orchard was so small as to make harvesting, except
for her own use, a complete waste of time. At the end of
her land she stopped for a breath. The fog had lifted
shortly after noon, and there was a sweet clean smell
about the earth. She rested one hand on the gnarled tree-

trunk nearest, and glared out to where another high-rise office building was under construction. Sacramento was surely expanding, like a rising loaf of bread gone mad.

Sunday was a lazy day. She slept late, then drove down into Rancho Cordova to St Clemens, the Episcopal Church on Zinfandel Drive. And then it was Monday.

'He wants you.' Betty Pervis, in early for a change, with a wide smirk on her face.

'He?' Phil struggled out of her jacket and swiped ineffectually at her fog-damped hair.

'Him. That Mr Wilderman.'

'What would he want me for? Don't tell me Mrs Simmons is out again?'

'No. I saw her come in twenty minutes ago. He wants you, Phil. I bet the minute he saw you he flipped.'

'Stop it, Betty. That's fairy-tale stuff. Besides, he never did see me. His eyes were bandaged all the time I was there.'

'Well,' the young girl pouted, 'it's happened before, you know.'

'What?' Phil was still trying vainly to control her curls. When wet they coiled up like little springs all over her head, and then jingled and bounced as she walked. 'What's happened before?'

'You know. The millionaire boss marries the typist?'

'Oh, sure he does. Daydreamer. So what did he say? What did he want?'

'I told you. He said he wanted you—and then he hung up like to burst my ear-drum. You'd better hurry up. He hates to be kept waiting.'

Mrs Simmons was in her appointed place, every iron-grey hair in place, her mannish tailored suit impeccable, her hands poised over the keys of her electronic typewriter. 'He wants you,' the older woman said, and nodded towards the door.

'That's getting to be the most hated quotation of the century,' Phil returned, smiling. 'He wants me for what?' Mrs Simmons shrugged her shoulders and smiled back. Phil shook her head in disgust and headed for the inner office.

His hearing must have improved. He heard the door as it opened. 'Well, damn it, isn't she here yet? How far is it to that typing pool?' A papa-bear growl, from an office almost as dim as a cave. He was at his desk. His son Robert was sitting on the divan in the corner. The boy got up silently, with not a wisp of a smile on his face.

'Yes, she's here.' Phil replied in her most serene tone. 'The typing pool is on the ground floor, a hundred miles from here.'

'Oh, a wit, no less,' he growled. Phil had already lost her desire to prick his bubble of conceit, regretted her poor attempt at humour.

'Well, you're half right,' she said wryly. She stood quietly in the middle of the room, eyes swerving from father to son, waiting. The boy was fidgeting, moving his weight from one foot to the other.

'Come over here.'

'Yes, Mr Wilderman——'

'Penn. Mr Wilderman is my father.'

Silence. Phil could think of nothing to say.

'You can't manage a simple name like that? Let me hear you say it. Penn.'

'I—Penn.'

'That's a start,' he laughed. His entire appearance changed. The worry-lines disappeared from his face,

taking years off his age. The dark glasses, sited at a
jaunty angle on the bridge of his nose, seemed to be
laughing at her. Not maliciously. Happily. Breathe, Phil
commanded herself, and relaxed as air poured into her
lungs. His fingers beckoned. She moved slowly towards
the desk until she was up to the typist's chair that stood
beside it.

'No further?' he asked.

'No.' It wasn't exactly a whisper, neither was it a full-
blown statement. I'm losing my nerve, Phil snarled at
herself.

He was up from his chair before she could assemble
her defences. Up and in front of her, inches away, with
both hands trapping her head between them. Fingers
moved up her cheeks, into her hair, and paused. Her
agitation ceased. The hands were stroking, calming.
Altogether—wonderful, she thought, and blushed at her
own statement.

'Good morning, Peabody,' he said softly. 'The records
tell me it's Philomena—is that right?'

Tongue-tied, Phil struggled to reply and gave up. His
fingers read her struggle, and moved down to cup her
chin. 'Do I frighten you?'

'Yes,' she managed. And then more bravely now that
the dam was broken, 'Yes. I wish you would stop pawing
me, Mr Wilderman—Penn. I——'

She managed to get to the chair as his hands dropped
away. That uneasy feeling crowded almost everything
else out of her mind. It bothered her because she could
not define it, and definition had circumscribed her life
for so long she felt lost.

'What do you want of me?' she asked impatiently.

He went back to his chair and sat down. He moved

with more confidence, more agility than he had the previous week, she thought. He stood a little taller, straighter, and there was an aura of power surrounding him. 'How are things in the typing pool?' he asked.

It was not what Phil had expected. She squared around in her chair, set both feet flat on the floor, and stiffened her spine. 'Work is slow,' she said in her office voice. 'On Monday it's always slow. By Tuesday, when the engineers have had a chance to think, work picks up.' And now what? Did he want to fire a couple of the girls? Save a little money in the over-inflated budget?

'That's good,' he said. Which again was not quite what she expected. Executives about to fire somebody don't usually start off with 'That's good'. She stole a quick glance at the boy. He had sat down when she did. Better manners she had never observed before in a teenager. And that was one of the problems. He was just too unnaturally quiet for an American teenager!

'We have a problem.' Penn broke in on her thoughts.

'*We* do?'

'Robert and I. We have a problem.' And I'll bet that's the understatement of the year, Phil told herself. She sat up even straighter, not willing to contribute a comment, and waited.

'You don't seem to care?'

'I'm sure you'll tell me about it when you're ready,' she returned primly. To emphasise the point she put her pencils away in her pocket and folded her hands in her lap. He cleared his throat, as if not accustomed to such rebuttal.

'Robert is growing out of all his clothes. You can see that, I suppose.'

'Yes.'

'I'm not boring you, am I, Philomena?'

'No, but nobody calls me that. I——'

'I should call you Miss Peabody? By the way, it *is* Miss, isn't it?'

'Yes. I mean, yes it is, not yes you should——' Another tangled tongue. She swallowed hard to clear the obstruction. 'I mean—you should call me Phil. And yes, it is *Miss* Peabody—Phil.'

'I'm glad we've settled that,' he chuckled. 'How in the world did you last as a *Miss* all this time? You seem to be a nice companionable lady.' Phil almost strangled over the words that wanted to pour out.

'Oh, never mind,' he conceded. 'None of my business, is it? What I want, Phil, is for you to take Robert out on the town this morning and get him a new outfit.'

'I——'

'No, I know it's not in the union contract. I'm asking for a favour.'

'I wasn't going to say that,' she retorted angrily. 'All I meant to say is I don't have any experience buying for men. All my expertise is with girls!'

'Boys, girls——' he grumbled. 'This is the unisex age. I don't see what difference that makes.'

'A lot you know,' Phil told him. 'The unisex age is almost over. The pendulum is swinging madly in the other direction. Girls look for the very feminine. Boys look for the very masculine.'

'And skirts are longer this year,' he chuckled. 'Or so they tell me. Why any woman with good-looking legs would want to wear skirts at mid-calf is more then I can reason out.'

'Perhaps that's to keep them from being ogled by men,' Phil said primly. 'And all that is beside the point. We were talking about Robert's clothes. He's old enough to pick out what he wants for himself. At most, you might have his mother go along with him to supervise.' A silence settled over the room. Penn Wilderman drubbed his fingers on his desktop. Robert Wilderman was staring at his father, his eyes wide open, and an anxious expression on his face.

'Robert,' the father finally broke the silence, 'would you please go out to Mrs Simmons' office for a moment. I need to speak privately to Peabody.'

'About my mother?' The belligerence was unmasked. The boy had no intention of sharing his mother's secrets with another woman, Phil thought, and he was making no bones about it.

'Robert!' A stern command that snapped like a whip, but left all the scars internally. The boy got up slowly from his chair, looked as if he might voice an objection, and thought better of it. He slammed the door behind him on the way out. The whole thing was too mediaeval for Phil to accept.

'I don't want to hear any of his mother's secrets,' she exploded. 'That's a terrible way to treat a child of his age. Terrible!'

'I didn't ask you in here to criticise my life-style—or my family's,' he snapped. 'Just shut up and sit down.'

'I am,' she fumed. 'And don't tell me to shut up. I can always get another job. Sacramento is crying out for experienced secretaries.' Just for emphasis she stuck her tongue out at him, and then had a hard time smothering the giggles brought on by her own silliness.

'I don't doubt you could get a hundred jobs,' he thundered. At least it seemed like thunder. It wasn't very loud, but it shook the furniture—and Phil—in a manner she was not eager to repeat. 'In fact, I might offer you a better job myself. Now just listen. OK?'

'OK,' she whispered, her fit of rebellion suppressed. Despite what she had said, it wasn't all *that* easy to get a new job—and she had worked for Pacific Mining for almost ten years now.

'My wife and I are divorced. Robert is our adopted child. My wife was awarded custody. Now my former wife has remarried and Robert had become an—obstruction, I guess you would say. So she shipped the boy to me, not even waiting to find out whether I was in the country or not. My son is a bright young man, but so thoroughly stamped down that he hardly appears normal. I'm sure you've seen that?'

'Yes,' she admitted. It was a hesitant agreement. His world of darkness seemed to be closing in on her, disordering her usually logical mind. Just for a minute she wished she had the nerve to get up and open a curtain. Outside the window Sacramento roared and chugged and whined its way into the future. Inside, she was swathed in a thousand veils that shrouded and blinded her to all but this man. This man who was suddenly turning from grouchy bully to loving, concerned father.

'So now I have a difficult problem,' he continued. 'I can't stand this man my wife—my former wife—has married, and I wouldn't want Robert to be within a hundred miles of them. Yet, to get the court order rescinded, I have to be able to provide a home life for him myself. And today is a beginning. You are obviously the motherly type. You don't think yourself too old for Robert?'

'Me?' she gulped. There it was again, that obsession he

seemed to have about age. 'Why—why no, I don't think of myself as too old for Robert, but I—I would hardly classify myself as a motherly type.'

'Come off it,' he chuckled. 'You brought up three girls——'

'Three sisters,' she insisted firmly. 'They were my younger sisters.'

'So all right, your younger sisters. Children none the less. You saw them through their scrapes and bruises and teens?'

'I—well, yes, so to speak.' It was technically not true. Sally was only eighteen—but his statement was close enough to the truth to be accepted.

'Then there you go,' he nodded. 'The motherly type. No, I don't see this as being any big thing. Your department is in the doldrums. You hop in the car, take Robert to some place where clothes can be had, and outfit him. Easy.'

'Not that easy,' she sighed. 'What sort of outfit? How many things? How much money are you willing to invest in all this? Children's clothes come higher priced than adult clothes these days.' Again that prim maiden-aunt tone. And I wish I could wash *that* out, she told herself fiercely.

'I want him to have a complete wardrobe,' Penn rumbled. 'It's up to you what he gets. As for money, there's a company credit card in my wallet here.' He squirmed around to reach his wallet out of his back pocket and laid it out on the desk. 'Take it with you. I don't really care how much things cost. Spend what you need to. Anything up to five hundred dollars, I would say. If you need more, give me a call from the store.'

Phil almost swallowed her tongue. Accustomed to

nursing money as if it were a sick relative, she could have outfitted three boys the size of Robert for five hundred dollars. And have change left over. She fumbled for the card.

'I—I guess I could manage,' she returned softly. 'I'll take him over to the K-street Mall in my car, and we'll——'

'Nonsense,' he said. Again that roll of thunder, that threat hanging in the background. 'My car is downstairs. Harry is probably ruining his lunch by chewing on doughnuts in the cafeteria. He'll drive you. Off you go.'

Off she went, indeed. It was like being swept out of the kitchen by a particularly big broom. Robert was standing at Mrs Simmons' desk, having said not a word, apparently. When she tapped him on the shoulder he followed. Not until they entered the lift did he speak.

'You're really going to buy me some clothes?'

That disdainful look, meaning *how can a mere female buy clothing for me?* His father's look all over again. The pair of them would be great candidates for monkhood, Phil told herself. I'd like to give them both a hot-foot to upset that darn dignity. How can a thirteen-year-old boy be such a stick? 'No,' she responded. 'I wouldn't dream of buying anything for you I'm going to take you somewhere where you can buy yourself some clothes— and your father's going to pay for them. Do you have any objection?'

He thought about it until they reached the lobby. 'No,' he said, as they stepped out of the lift.

A short bandy-legged man was leaning against the reception desk. He looked like an out-of-work jockey with grey hair and no semblance of uniform. When he saw Robert he sauntered over to them, spread both feet apart, and issued a challenge.

'You the broad gonna take Robbie shopping?'

She glared at him, eyeball to eyeball. It wasn't hard. They were both about the same height. 'Yes,' she snapped. 'I'm the—er—broad that is taking Robert shopping. Are you Harry?'

'Who else?' he sighed. Another woman-hater, Phil noted. That makes three. They must be a close tribe, the Wildermans. I wonder if there are any more at home? 'Well, c'mon,' the little man drawled, 'I don't have all day.'

'Do you not really?' Phil drawled in return. 'Have to get your bets in at the track, do you?'

'Well,' he stuttered, embarrassed by her directness. 'I—hey, the car's out front in a no-parking zone.'

'Where else?' She did her best to present a royal cold stare, but just the doing broke her up. When she giggled he smiled back at her. Out of the corner of her eye she could see the boy smiling too.

The car was one of those stretch-Cadillacs, two blocks long, with shaded windows for one-way viewing. Hollywood style. Phil classified it all as she scrambled into the back seat. Robert dithered a moment or two, and then desire overcame manners. He scrambled in up front, next to the driver. Mark it down, Phil, her subconscious demanded. He's really a thirteen-year-old kid. Give him the chance and he'd have the engine out and in pieces on the pavement. All that dignity is faked!

'Where to?' The little man needed a pillow under him to see over the steering-wheel. His voice had the gravel-sound of those who do a great deal of shouting in their lives. 'Where to, Miss——?'

'Peabody,' Robert told him, using his father's inflection.

'To the lower K-street Mall,' she said. ' I don't rightly know how you'll get there. They're tearing up that whole area to put in the Light Rail vehicles, and——'

'I know,' Harry grunted. 'Been drivin' in this town for twenty years or more.' That seemed to be that. Phil buttoned her lip and relaxed into the soft springy seat, planning her strategy. Unfortunately she found it hard to give Robert's needs her full attention. His father's face seemed to haunt her. *And I don't know when I've met a more despicable man*, she insisted to herself.

Harry proved to be some sort of driving genius. He managed to deliver them to the back of the Mall without scraping a fender, or killing anyone in the middle of the mad traffic jam which normally haunted the Capitol Mall when the California legislature were in session. Phil began to breathe again when Harry pulled over to the kerb in a no-waiting zone and opened the door.

'Lose your breath, lady?' he asked as he handed her out.

'I always do when someone else is driving,' she apologised. A real smile was her reward. 'I don't know how long we'll be,' she hazarded. He shrugged his shoulders.

'Makes no mind,' he returned. 'I'll be around here somewheres. You come out, I'll find you.' Robert climbed out without assistance and stood fidgeting, as if he had never been in downtown Sacramento before.

'Over this way,' she called, and led him across the grass and tree-lined open mall. Her goal was the classic simplicity of Macy's, but before they made it to the front doors the boy stopped and stared.

'What's that?' he asked in awe. Phil looked up. As a perennial shopper she tended to ignore the obvious these days. The boy was standing almost underneath the Indo Arch, a mass of steel formed vaguely in the pointed-arch shape of an Indian Temple door. Soaring forty feet above the surrounding mall, it was the starkly symbolic gate between the modern State capital and the rebuilt park area known as Old Sacramento.

'You've never been here before?' she asked.

'I've never been anywhere around here,' he returned bitterly. 'There never was any time. My—she was always busy at something or other. She never had time.'

How about that? Phil mused. She spent a few minutes explaining about the arch, and the reconstructed Old Sacramento.

'I'd like to see that some day,' he said. Not enthusiastically, just a general comment. Which made it even more strange to her when she heard herself say, 'Maybe we could come. I'd be glad to take you.'

He looked at her as if she were some curious sea-monster. As if he had heard but could not believe. 'You mean that?'

'I said it,' she said grimly, wishing she could take it all back. They marched into the store without another word. From long practice, Phil knew her way around. She led him unhesitatingly to the Men and Boys clothing area, and then stopped him with a small hand on his wrist.

'Now you have to decide just what you want to wear,' she told him. He was the slightest bit taller than she, and it was unnerving to see how his grey eyes studied her. I wonder what colour his father's eyes are, she pondered as he thought out an answer.

'You really mean that? I can decide for myself?'

'Why not? You have to live in them. What's your favourite?'

'Jeans,' he replied immediately. So what else is new, Phil chuckled to herself. Give a kid enough rope and he'll buy—blue jeans. She waved her hand towards the proper aisles, and followed as he plunged down them like a young colt just unleashed into fresh pastures. Jeans. They come in all size and all styles and all colours, and he just couldn't make up his mind.

'If you're sure of the size,' she prompted, 'try on one pair, and then take a couple of each.' That broke the log-jam. He actually smiled. With his whole face *and* his eyes, he smiled. As with his father, it changed his whole appearance. The solemn formal stick figure turned into a glowing teenager. He was gone into a fitting-booth before Phil could add another word.

She sank into a chair, glad to rest her feet. If this expedition were to be anything like a shopping trip with her sisters, she would need arch-supporters before the day was done. It was—pleasant—just to sit there, watching people buzz around her like a hive of angry yellow-jackets. She was surprised when Robert came out of the booth and stood in front of her.

'Do you think this would do?' he asked hesitantly. She smothered her smile. This was not the time for it. The waist band was comfortably loose, although the jeans clung to him like a second skin. The legs were a little too long, but a quick needle would turn up the cuffs with ease.

'Do you like them?' she countered.

He strutted back and forth, did a couple of deep knee bends, all without bursting out of the pants, and then came back. The smile was flickering, as if he expected a denial. 'I like them,' he said fiercely.

'So we'll get—oh—six pairs,' she commented casually. 'Choose the rest of them, but make sure they're this same size.'

He flashed away again, thumbing through the racks as if he were a seasoned shopper. In fifteen minutes he had accumulated an armful, and the smile seemed permanently fixed.

'And now shirts, socks, and underwear,' she announced. He nodded happily. 'And one suit, for dress-up.' She expected rage, and got acquiescence. It took another hour to complete his outfit. The credit card was somewhat more worn than when she first received it. *But*, Phil told herself, *if it were Sally, we would have one dress by now, and I'd be exhausted.*

It was warm outside. The sun had finally broken through and dried off the fog. Aircraft seemed to be stacked to preposterous heights, waiting to be called in to the landing pattern of the Metropolitan Airport, to their north. A few pigeons, paying absolutely no attention to the sanitation rules, were dive-bombing the pedestrians. And Harry was waiting for them beside the Arch.

'Bought a lot, did you?' the little man asked. For some reason the gravelly voice seemed more friendly than before. He came up to Phil and relieved her of all her packages, without offering help to the boy at all. *And he's doing that on purpose*, she told herself. Robbie was tired. She could read that on his face. But there was a stubborn determination there too. The first one to offer him help would get a first-class set-down! But women are entitled to be tired, she chuckled to herself, and put on such a demonstration that they both believed it.

The ride back was different. When Phil climbed in to

the back seat, Robbie was close behind her. Harry took the long-cut, around the Capitol building and the park that lay behind it, then wandering eastward past the reconstruction of Sutter's Fort, north around the cool green of McKiney Park, east again to circle the scattered buildings of the Sacramento branch of the University of California, and then back in a twisting path through the back streets, until they were in front of the Pacific Mining and Metals building.

'Leave them packages in the car,' Harry instructed.

'Someone has to do a little sewing on the trouser legs,' Phil told him. 'They need to be taken up about an inch. Can you get it done?' He looked doubtful, but helped her out of the car and then drove off.

'I know your mother would have been a better help for you,' she told the boy. His face hardened. She fumbled to a stop.

The boy was bursting with something he wanted to say. It tumbled out in all the bitterness of a thirteen-year-old mind. 'My mother hates me,' he announced, and strode off towards the front door of the building.

'Now wait just a darn minute,' she called after him. He stopped. She walked over to confront him. 'Don't you ever say anything like that,' she lectured. 'You don't know everything there is to know about your mother and the world. What do you suppose your father would say if he heard that!'

The boy was close to tears, but his pride was bigger than his frame. 'He wouldn't care,' he said. 'He hates me too.'

CHAPTER THREE

PHIL made sure that Robbie got to the right lift, then turned back and hurried to the typing pool. It was after one, and the girls were gradually drifting back to work. 'While the cat's away, huh?' She grinned at them and headed for her own work station. A surprising amount of work had come in, for a Monday morning. She thumbed through it all and made a distribution among them.

'Not El Dorado again,' Harriet groaned as she scanned her assigned workload. 'It's a devil of a note when a company can't take gold out of its own mine!'

'Type,' Phil chuckled. 'Yours not to reason why. El Dorado county had become a suburb since the old days. The new residents are householders, not old miners. You can't blame them for not wanting us to reactivate the old mines.'

'I can,' Harriet returned. 'I don't make enough money to move out there. Why should I feel sorry for them? They work on the idea that *I've got mine, and to hell with anybody else*. They don't want to listen to the fact that the mines on the Mother Lode were there before *they* were.'

'Oh, wow,' Phil laughed. 'That sounds definitely like sour grapes. Or is it Lionel again?'

Harriet waved her comment aside. 'Lionel is long gone,' she said, bending over her word-processor keyboard. 'It's Frank now. And yes, he's a pain in my—stomach. Oooh!'

'Oooh?'

38

'Look who just came in!'

Phil whirled around. The entire room was quiet. Only one keyboard clicked. Penn Wilderman stood at the door, his hand resting lightly on Harry's shoulder. It was the first time she had seen him in full light. His face, screened by the inevitable dark glasses, was narrower than she had thought. The black hair tumbled in some profusion, to curl slightly at the back of his neck. He went from broad shoulders to narrow hips, reminding Phil of the boy. There was an aura about him, a feeling of poise, of command. His grey three-piece suit was immaculate. His tie, slightly loosened, flamed red against the white of his shirt. Not a huge man, not at all, but big enough.

Harry led him down the narrow aisle that separated the work positions. 'Peabody?' Penn said.

'Yes?' Her stomach quivered. She took a deep breath to calm it. You've been doing a lot of that lately, her conscience nagged.

'Lunch,' he announced. The keys in the background stopped clicking, as all the typists listened unabashedly.

'I—I have a packed lunch,' she stammered. 'The boy——'

'The boy is on his way home to try out his new clothes. And now you and I are lunching. There's something I want to talk over with you.'

'Oh!' Well, what else do you say? To Phil's certain knowledge the boss of Pacific Mining had never ever come down into the typing pool. Neither father nor son. And now, oh so casually, *lunch!*

'Mr Wilderman——'

'Penn.'

'Ah—er—Penn. I don't go out for lunch, and it's——'

'I know. It's not in the union contract. But you'll come anyway because it's a favour.'

'I—yes.' It wasn't a question of making up her mind. That area was totally vacant, spinning around in an upset such as her twenty-seven years had not known before. And tumbling out of the vacuum her voice had given its own answer.

His hand transferred to her shoulder. 'Get the car, Harry,' he ordered, and then urged Phil down the aisle towards the door. Behind them a buzz of conversation rose. 'They'll have enough gossip to last a week,' he told her softly as the door sighed shut behind them.

'Well, I don't relish being the subject of it,' she grumbled. His hand squeezed her shoulder—partly warning, partly command. She stepped off briskly towards the front door.

His magic carpet of a Cadillac whisked them over to L street in a matter of minutes, and into Frank Fat's restaurant, the favourite eatery of the Republican administration. He must have called ahead. A table was waiting for them. They moved through the crush like an elephant train, first the *maître d'*, then Phil, and slightly behind her, hand on her shoulder for a guide, Penn. He seemed to have a good many friends in the late-lunch crowd. People called out to him from both sides as they passed, but he signalled her forward.

'I'm really hungry,' he said as he fumbled at the back of her chair, then trailed a hand around the table to the opposite side. 'The Beaumonts quit this morning. That's the third couple I've lost in six weeks.'

'I'm not surprised,' she muttered.

'What?'

'I said I'm surprised,' she lied cheerfully. The frown on

his face indicated disbelief.

'Yes, well—I want the steak, please. The special, with onions and oyster sauce. Philomena?'

'Please,' she cringed. 'Someone might hear you. Phil is my name. And I couldn't possibly—oh, bring me the Chef's Salad, please, and a cup of tea.'

'Now, where was I?'

'The Beaumonts quit this morning?'

'Yes. And Harry is such a terrible cook.'

'Didn't you know that slavery is against the law? It seems to me that Harry is around day and night.'

He smiled at her, tilting his head in a truly attractive move. 'Harry and I go a long way back,' he told her. 'He's one of my father's old war buddies. I think he's shared everything I've ever done—except for Vietnam. Ah, I love the smell of Fat's steak special. Sure you won't have some?'

'Of course not,' she sighed. 'I'd be a balloon in three weeks if I ate like that.' After a moment she stopped eating, staring at his dexterity. He attacked his food with vigour—just as he does everything else, she thought. That hank of black hair kept sliding down over his forehead. Phil squeezed her own hands together to get rid of that traitorous impulse. Leaning across a table to brush the hair out of his eyes was just too much to expect of an employee!

He managed about half of his steak, then laid his utensils aside and dabbed at his mouth with his napkin. 'Well?'

She was caught by surprise again, idly tracing the line of his chin with her eyes. 'Well? Well what?'

'So are you going to help us?'

'I—I guess I don't understand, Mr—er—Penn.'

'Robert and Harry and I are living in a big house. We need help.'

'Oh. Yes, I suspect you do. You want me to find another couple to take care of the house, is that it? I'm not really in the personnel business, but I suppose I could ask around and see if something can be arranged. There must be *somebody* willing to put up with you!'

And there goes your big mouth, she yelled at herself. What sort of a way is that to talk to your boss? *Somebody might be willing to put up with you. Hah!* 'I—I really didn't mean that, Mr Wilderman,' she stammered. 'I don't know what came over me.'

'I do,' he rumbled. 'You've got a terminal case of honesty. That's one of the several things about you that I like.'

'But——' She gave thanks again that he couldn't see her mad blushes. If there were anything about herself that she hated, it was that blood-surging blush that gave her away in many a tight corner.

He was off on his own hobby-horse. 'I like you because you're quiet,' he enumerated. 'You tell me the truth. You are eminently practical. You know how to handle children. You know how to handle grouches and bullies. You know how to handle other women. You're a fine figure of a woman. And you're old enough not to be bothered with all this first flush of love and emotion. You are altogether a fine person, Philomena.'

Her first confused reaction was, 'Hush, people are listening'. And then her flustered mind marshalled all his statements, everything seemed fine until she ran into *and you're old enough to*—that was the phrase that stuck in her craw. She threw up her hands in disgust, and pushed her plate away.

'Finished eating?' He had returned to the work at hand, and was proving to be a fine trencherman.

'Yes,' she sighed. She put both elbows on the table and rested her chin on them, trying to read his face. She waited until he had completely dismantled the lunch, and then, 'Just what is it you want me to do?' She tried to keep her voice cool and low. The couple at the next table were taking an inordinate interest in *their* discussion.

'Simple,' he said. 'I want you to come live with us.'

'You want me to *what*!'

'Hey, keep your voice down,' he chuckled. 'We don't want everybody in the place to know what we're talking about, do we?'

'I—no!' Phil collapsed back into her chair and dabbed at the residue of the overturned water glass, a victim of her outraged jump to her feet. 'No.' More softly, but hissing with her anger. 'Say that again. You want me to what?'

'I said, we want you to come and live with us. Surely for someone of your age and charm that's not a surprise?'

'Well, a lot you know,' she hissed back at him. 'What has my age and charm got to do with it! I——'

'All right. Don't blow a fuse. It's not all that complicated. I thought you wouldn't mind coming over and looking after our house—and us. You have kept house before, haven't you?'

'Yes,' she snapped, 'for my own family. All girls. And you have the nerve to—I——'

'I didn't think it took a great deal of nerve.' She flashed a look. His face was solemn. There might be laughter behind the words, but his face was solemn. Her hand waved in her natural gesture, and she looked at the upset glass by her plate.

'I—you startled me,' she sighed. 'I spilled——'

'I hope it's water,' he interrupted. 'It's running down the leg of my trousers.'

'Oh, my,' Phil gasped. She snatched at the two other place napkins and rushed around to his side, madly sponging at his trouser-leg.

'I think I'd rather be wet than notorious,' he grumbled. 'I suppose now that everyone in the restaurant is looking at us?' Phil's empty hand flew to her mouth as she straightened up and glanced around. Everyone was. Clutching desperately at the wet napkins she sidled around the table and back to her seat.

'I—I'm sorry.' She had to make do with a whisper. It was all that would come out. 'They're all—staring. I'm sorry!'

'For God's sake,' he returned. 'I'm not asking you to give up the world and enter into seclusion. You have a holiday coming, don't you.'

'I—yes. Four weeks. But I thought I would save it for the summer, and then I could help my sisters with——'

'So give me two weeks of it now. Your job will be protected for you—and at the end of that time we could see how it's going.'

'I——' She closed her mouth with a snap. If I give him a word off the top of my head I'll regret it, she thought. It's too easy to say yes to this—this aggravating man. He seems to have some sort of mind-control over me. Or have I been missing someone to care for these days? All I know is that I want to say *yes*, but I'd better not! So she compromised.

'I think that's too much for a quick decision. Mr Wilderman—er—Penn. I'll have to think it over very carefully.'

'Why?' He was going to pound at her defences, and she grew more wary because of that. 'You know me. I'm the world's biggest grouch, right?' Phil shook her head in agreement, and then thanked heaven that he couldn't see. 'Are you afraid of me?' She shook her head again. 'Can't say anything?'

'I—it's Robert I don't know. He could be a bigger problem than all three of my sisters combined.'

'I don't see why you say that. He's just a normal thirteen-year-old kid.'

'Hah! A lot you know!' She hadn't meant to say that. It slipped out. But having said it, the rest had to follow. 'Robert is a mixed-up child. He thinks his mother hates him.'

'She does. Almost as much as she hates me. That woman would do anything in the world to do me in. Well, maybe that's an exaggeration. I think she would draw the line at hiring a hit-man to get rid of me. That would be like killing the chicken that lays the golden eggs.'

'Goose,' she advised absent-mindedly. 'Goose that laid the golden eggs.'

'Yeah,' he noted. 'Our divorce settlement gave her a quarter share in Pacific Mining.'

'I—but a mother can hardly hate her own child. That's just biologically not an in-thing.'

'Robbie is an adopted child,' he reminded her. A chill seemed to gather around Phil's heart. The way he talked about his wife was pure venom. But this casual reference to Robbie was like a chunk of ice. *It's true*, she told herself. *He hates the boy too! And they look so much alike. Carbon copies. His illegitimate child?*

'I—I need to think about it,' she maintained stubbornly. His sigh shook them both.

'All right.' He wadded up his napkin and threw it down. 'Then there's no need for us to remain here, is there?' He hardly waited for an answer, but scraped his chair back and stood up. The waiter hurried over.

'Madame did not care for her lunch?'

'What the hell—didn't you eat anything?'

'I wasn't hungry,' Phil said quietly. The waiter held her chair as she stood up. 'Shall we go now?' She moved over to him, and lifted his hand to her shoulder. It lay there for a second, and then closed in a harsh grip that hurt her. He seemed to be in the grip of some strong emotion. She bore it until a whimper was forced out of her, at which point the grip relaxed. No apology came. Phil struggled to control her facial muscles. It would be adding to the gossip if she led him through the crowd with tears in her eyes. He waited patiently.

The Cadillac carried them painlessly back to the office building, where Penn scrambled out. Phil followed, helping him to the door. 'The reception people will take me the rest of the way,' he said gruffly. 'You go home. You've some considerable thinking to do.'

'But it's only two-thirty,' she said. Being late, quitting early, shirking the hard jobs—these were just not the things that the Philomenas of the world did. But he insisted.

'I do believe I have a little influence with your boss. That's Henderson, isn't it—in Administration?'

'Yes. I had to take two days off for my sister's wedding, and Mr Henderson won't like it if——'

'Mr Henderson will think it's just grand,' he chuckled. 'He'll be so pleased he'll do handsprings. Go home. Harry?' The wiry little man came over to them. 'Harry, take Miss Peabody to her car. And while you're at it, check the damn thing over. I hear that most women in this town drive junk.'

'Well, I really——' Phil stamped her foot and prepared to give him a piece of her mind, but it was too late. He went through the doors, and the two receptionists were fawning all over him. Just watching turned Phil's stomach.

So, like Cinderella, Phil rode around the corner in great style, to be deposited beside her rusty old car. The coach had turned into a pumpkin faster than any fairy godmother could swing a wand. Harry got out with her and circled the ancient Subaru, making *tch tch* noises as he went. Phil stood by the driver's door, key in hand, waiting as if she expected a death sentence from him.

'It's an old car,' he commented as he came up to her.

'I know that.' It's hard not to *sound* exasperated when one is. She did her best, but he caught the inflection.

'If it was a horse we would've shot it four years ago.'

'You don't have to be a critic,' she snapped.

'Brakes work OK?'

'Of course they do.' Righteous indignation, followed by an immediate amendment, because the truth must be served. 'Well, perhaps they're a little bit—soft?'

'Turn on the engine.'

She slid into the driver's seat, flustered, and was unable to find the ignition lock. 'Take your time,' he offered sarcastically. Which made her angry enough to do just that.

The key finally achieved its purpose. The engine rumbled, turned over a couple of times, and then caught with a ragged roar. The car body shook, It was all so normal that Phil smiled. Until the little man stuck his head in the car window.

'Four-cylinder engine?'

'Yes!'

'Only runnin' on three. Been that way a long time, I suppose?'

'I—leave me alone,' she muttered as she reached for the gear-lever. He backed away, looking as if it would all blow up when she moved it.

'Lights work?' he yelled as she moved slowly out of her parking slot.

'Yes,' she roared back at him. It was a definite lie, but since she never drove after dark, she felt it could be marked down as a minor misdemeanour. She snatched a quick look at him in the rear-view mirror. He was laughing.

'Darn nuisance,' she muttered as she turned right on Fifteenth Street and headed for Route 50. During the entire trip home to Rancho Cordova she spent ninety per cent of her time painting images of the jockey and his boss in her mind, and throwing mental darts at them. Which left only ten per cent of her brain to navigate the car—about par for the course with California drivers.

The car squealed to a halt in the familiar driveway, throwing up pebbles and dust in all directions. She got out and walked around the steaming vehicle, trying to see what Harry had seen. It wasn't hard. She was driving a piece of junk, she told herself. She kicked at the left tyre to relieve her anger.

Supper was as simple as one could get. Two fried eggs shoved into a sandwich, and a glass of cold milk to go with it. Then back out to the living-room to ponder. Channel 13 news was on. She watched it with half an eye, deep in thought. Come live with me. Of course, he didn't mean it the way it sounded. Give up your typing job, and come and be my housekeeper was what he meant. Which gave it all an entirely different slant. She loved her job. On the other hand there was something to be said for staying at home and keeping house. *I wonder where he lives. What* kind *of a house is it that needs keeping?* The questions piled up, while the answers receded.

Along about ten o'clock the telephone ruined her chances to see—again—the old black and white movie, *Raffles*. She snapped off the set with a twinge of regret and went out into the hall to answer the call.

'Phil, this is Debbie.' Phil groaned, Debbie lived about five miles away, on the edge of Fair Oaks, and only called when she wanted something. As in this case.

'Phil—John and I have a chance to take a wonderful trip up to Tahoe on the weekend, but we can't take the girls!' *I'll bet you can't*, Phil thought. *Two more monstrous kids I've never seen. Real hell-raisers.* 'So we thought we'd let their aunt really get to know them,' Debbie continued. 'How about if I bring them over on Friday night, and we'll pick them up Sunday night late?'

And that will shoot my weekend for sure, Phil thought. *A whole lovely weekend baby-sitting for somebody else's children. So their aunt can get to know them? Their aunt knows all she wants to know about them. They expect me to clothe them and feed them and nurse them, and nobody will ever say a word about payment.*

John is a senior architect, and they're looking for a free baby-sitter! Good old dependable Phil! It was hard to tell which one of the sisters was most surprised at the answer. The little family push had been just enough to make up Phil's mind for her. She would accept Penn Wilderman's offer—because she was curious, and to please herself for a change. Just herself, no one else. Because she wanted to find out what would happen. And here was the perfect opportunity to burn her boats before she could change her mind back again.

'I'm really sorry,' she said, 'but I won't be available this weekend.'

'Oh, Phil!' Under the usual procedure. Debbie would cry a little, Phil would simmer, and then relent. *Not this time, sister.* 'But Phil, we counted on you!'

'How about the week after?'

'Not then either, Debbie. Why don't you hire a baby-sitter! There are plenty available.'

Deep silence from the other end, then an off-telephone conference. John came on the line. 'Phil, you just have to do this for us. Debbie needs a vacation, and——'

'So do I, John. I haven't had one in ten years. But I intend to take one now.'

'Hey Phil, what's got into you?'

'It's hard to tell.' She managed to work up a chuckle. 'But whatever it is, I like it. Do have a good time, John. Call me when you get back and tell me all about it—oops. I forgot. I won't be here. Well, I'll be in touch.' She laid the receiver down on to its cradle with a broad smile on her face. Her brother-in-law was still spluttering as she disconnected.

'One nail in my coffin,' she teased herself as she went for coffee. 'Now, if the family grapevine is working——'

It was. No sooner had she made her mug of instant coffee and added the skimmed milk than the telephone rang again. *They'll push me over the top, to where I can't possibly back out!* She smiled as she picked up the instrument.

'Phil, just what are you up to?' Imperious Samantha.

Being a doctor's wife was next door to coronation in Sam's mind.

'Up to?' Phil queried. 'Why, I can't honestly say that I'm up to anything much. What makes you ask?'

'Debbie called me. She's all upset, Phil.'

'Is she really? How terrible.'

'Phil, you *are* up to something. I can smell it.'

That's some nose. Phil wanted to say, but didn't. Samantha and her husband lived downtown, adjacent to Mercy Hospital, more miles away than the crows cared to fly in a California winter.

'I can't imagine what gave you that idea,' Phil coaxed. 'The truth of the matter is that I'm tired of having all of you lean on me, Sam. I almost feel as if my life stopped when Mother died—and I took her place. Now it's ten years later, I'm twenty-seven, and people treat me as if I were fifty. I want something more out of life, Sam.'

'Phil! You've lost your head! And besides—what will we all do without you?'

For the first time a serious note crept into Phil's voice. 'Why, I guess you'll all learn to grow up just a little bit more,' she sighed. She was going to have to use stronger ammunition to make them see things her way, Phil decided. And the language they all understand and respect is: 'I've found a man,' she said softly. Her sister made a curious noise at the other end of the telephone and hung up.

'And now,' Phil announced to the house at large, 'they'll both be over here tomorrow to bring me back to the straight and narrow. But neither of them gets up early enough to catch me before I go off to work, so all I really need to do is be gone by the end of the day. The coward's way out, Philomena. Just exactly what I need!' That night, still dithering, she packed a bag. And so to bed.

The day blessed her decision. The sun was up bright and clear. The early morning fog had dissipated before seven o'clock. The highways were cluttered, but not jammed. One or two dare-devil sparrows could be heard above the hum of civilisation. Phil started earlier than usual, just in case either of her sisters made the supreme sacrifice. Which was just as well.

The doors to the building were already unlocked, but nobody was in reception, and the typing pool was still locked. She fumbled with her key and propped the door open while she felt the inside wall for the light switch. The rows of fluorescent lights flared. And the voice at her elbow said, 'Miss Peabody, they don't fit.'

She dropped her bag, startled, and whirled around. Robert was directly behind her, a rebellious look on his face. A dirty face, at that.

'What don't fit?' She was struggling for time. Never an early-morning person, Phil required a little prompting to get moving.

'The trousers. They don't fit.'

'But that's only the cuff,' she said solemnly. 'I told you yesterday. Every pair of jeans has to be turned up. It won't take but a minute or two with a sewing machine, and not more than ten to fifteen minutes by hand.'

'Really?' A faint appeal stalked that thin face. *And that's something I can do for him*, Phil told herself fiercely. *He hasn't an ounce of confidence in himself! Or anyone else, for that matter!*

'Really,' she repeated. 'What did your father——'

'His father said why didn't you stop at the tailor's.' Penn Wilderman came stalking in from out of the dimly lit lobby. 'So why didn't you.'

'Because I don't think Macy's has a tailor on tap,' she said fiercely. 'And even if they did, this isn't the sort of thing you need a tailor for. Anybody can sew a cuff. Anybody!'

When he laughed she knew he was laughing at himself, and her happy grin flashed back at him. 'Evidently not quite everybody,' he returned. 'I tried last night, and Harry did too.' He looked down at her with his head tilted—that crazy boyish look on his face—and only the dark glasses to distort the happy picture. She was mesmerised by that smile. It tugged at her heart, and her head had no chance.

The water's too deep, she whispered to herself. Way over my head. But she dived in anyway. 'When we get home tonight I'll fix it,' she said.

CHAPTER FOUR

PENN allowed Phil all morning to straighten out the affairs of the typing pool, and to leave Harriet a notebook full of advice. That, of course, left her no time to call either of her sisters. Which helped her guilt feelings immensely. They could hardly interfere when they knew nothing about what was happening. Robbie, demonstrating his confidence in absolutely nobody, sat near her in the work-room. 'To make sure I don't escape?' she asked him.

He returned a tiny smile, and continued to play around with one of the spare word-processors. He did generate a little stir when, along about ten-thirty, he managed to break the corporation's access code and went wheeling and dealing among the corporate memories. Phil caught the action out of the corner of her eye and hustled over to him.

She leaned over his shoulder and turned off the set. 'And just what do you think you're up to, young man?'

'Nothing.' He sat there rigidly, hands still on the keyboard.

'Nothing? That access code is designed especially to keep people out of our records.'

He swivelled around in his chair and looked up at her. His narrow face was flushed. 'It's a stupid code,' he announced. 'Any *hacker* could solve it in twenty minutes.'

'But you took a whole hour?'

'Well, I'm only thirteen, for goodness' sake. What do you expect of a kid?'

'Yeah, kid,' she chuckled. 'Don't do it again—today, that is. Promise?'

He studied her for a moment, looking for—something. 'Well, OK. Promise.' And still those eyes staring, judging. Phil walked away, trying to look confident, but actually keeping her fingers crossed. *Too bright,* she told herself. *He may be adopted, but he's a chip off the old block for all that. What am I letting myself in for?*

There was no more time to ponder. Penn arrived at eleven o'clock. Phil was not watching, but the sudden silence was enough to announce his appearance. She finished the sentence, gave Harriet a quick 'God bless', and headed for the door.

'I have my car in the car park,' she said. 'I'll follow you.'

'Suitcases?'

'In the boot.'

'Harry, transfer the suitcases and have someone bring her car along. Robbie's waiting in the limousine, Peabody. Let's get a move on.'

She was still fumbling with 'But I' when they reached the lobby, his hand firmly on her shoulder. Harry had already disappeared. They were out on the pavement before she could muster up a 'This isn't right.' And even then it hardly contained enough indignation to make it worth while. He pulled her to a halt. 'The flowers,' he asked brusquely. 'What kind?'

She sniffed the air. From long usage she had forgotten them, sited in large pots on either side of the entrance inside the lobby.

'Camellias,' she said. 'It's like a little artificial garden.

Your father loves them, they say. The gardener keeps
changing them whenever the cold gets to them. There's a
greenhouse somewhere. Haven't you ever been here
before?'

'Not me,' he laughed. 'I was always the kid they sent
out into the field. When my father decided I was
seasoned enough to run the company I was no longer
interested. I wouldn't have come back—except my
mother laid it out for me, too. A very domineering
woman, my mother. Come on.'

'Wait,' she said softly, and slipped out from under his
hand. The blooms were profuse. She picked one of them
and was back at his side.

'Now what?'

'Stand still,' she ordered, stretching for his lapel.
'Darn. You modern men have ruined a good custom. No
button hole in your lapel. Here, I'll tuck them into your
jacket pocket.' His warm hand closed over hers and
carried both up to his lips. It was a fleeting kiss. Just a
touch of warmth that made her shiver. 'You're a strange
one, Peabody,' he chuckled. 'Whoever would have
thought? Flowers in February. I'll have all my suits
altered. Button holes coming up!'

'Now *you're* being silly,' she laughed. 'Robbie is
getting impatient. Come on.' As they went across the
wide walkway she kept cadence to herself, 'Button holes,
button holes, button holes.' And for some strange reason
it warmed her heart.

The ride was smooth, like drifting in a canoe down a
slow-moving river. It was comfortable, too. She was in
between Robbie and his father, and the width of the seat
provided plenty of room. 'As soon as we get home I need
you to put those drops in my eyes,' he said as they circled

around down the one-way maze that led to Fifteenth Street.

Phil had already lost track of their route. 'Does it hurt much?'

'Hardly,' he grunted.

'And you can't see a thing?'

'Hey, don't work up that pity bit,' he chuckled. 'I can see. Shapes, outlines—but everything is a little fuzzy. It's getting better. The doctor says it's sort of like getting a bad sunburn. Another three weeks and I'm sure everything will be cleared up. These pads are just a precaution.'

'That's a relief.'

'You were worried about my dad?' The boy was trying to puzzle something out.

'Of course I was worried.' Phil tried to keep it all on a casual basis, but for some reason that was becoming a hard thing to do.

'But two weeks ago you didn't even know him.' The boy had the bit in his teeth, and meant to run with it.

'That doesn't stop me from worrying now that I *do* know him.'

'You're funny.'

Penn's hand came over and squeezed hers. *A warning, or a comfort? Maybe both?* At least I can hope, she thought.

They were in a part of Sacramento Phil had never seen. A little enclave of winding roads, scattered houses. A sign said South Land Park Drive. Another, swathed in old trees, said 12th Street. Directly ahead was the Sacramento River, masked by the trees. They were in the old section of the city, where residential land sold by the foot, not by the quarter-acre. They turned left.

'You don't live here?' A hesitant question begging for denial.

'I believe I do,' Penn answered.

'But—this is where all the millionaires live!'

'I do believe you're right.'

'I——' The car turned off the street, through a set of wrought-iron gates that opened on a small circular drive. A stone wall circled the block-long property. Bushes and trees hid the house from the street. The car came to a stop in front of a massive building that sparkled with windows.

'You don't live here!' An angry statement, defying an answer.

'I do believe I do.'

'Well!' A large sigh to accompany. 'How in the world do you think I can housekeep such a monstrous house all my myself?'

'My mother did.'

'Well, she must have been some sort of—I don't believe it. It's just not possible. For a house like this you have to hire half a dozen servants!'

He was pushing her out. 'Not quite. Only five, I think!'

'But you—you—said that Mr and Mrs Beaumont had quit and that you wanted me to——' She turned around and faced up to him. Nose to chest, so to speak. The closer she got the taller he seemed to be. 'I think you had better tell me just what you want *me* for, Mr Wilderman!'

'To fix my trousers,' Robbie answered from behind her.

'That's one good reason,' Penn chuckled. 'There are half a dozen more. What I really want is for you to get these people of ours organised so there's some order and efficiency and quiet in this crazy house. I don't expect you to peel the potatoes and make the soup or sweep the floor. Organisation, Philomena!'

'Oh!' She bit at her lip, wished that her car were there for a quick get-away, and alternately wished she had worn sharp-pointed shoes, so she might kick him in the ankle.

'Now, shall we go in?' He tucked his hand under her elbow to emphasise the fact that the invitation was purely rhetorical. The house was a stranger to the Sacramento area. Built along the lines of an old Spanish *hacienda*, it would have fitted better into the softer climate of southern California. But the walls, the trees, the isolation, hid it from all its neighbours, of whom there were few. Pillared arches provided a porch, and swept around the sides of the house to form an open mall. The house itself was deep-set within this portico, with wide arched windows flanked by huge wooden shutters. Around the entire second floor a narrow balcony ran, railed with filigree iron. Phil could barely see the curved red tiles of the roof, topped with four sets of twin chimneys. Penn seemed to read her mind.

'Conspicuous consumption,' he said. 'My great-grandfather had it built, when gold was still pouring out of the Mother Lode. Impressed?'

'Frightened,' Phil returned. 'I just keep wondering what happens to me at midnight. Pumpkins and mice?'

He chuckled and hurried her into the house. Robbie trailed behind them, while Harry struggled with her bags. A young girl was waiting for them in the bright hall. Seventeen, perhaps, or eighteen. Short curly black hair, held precariously in place by a white ribbon. A round full face, with smooth tan complexion. Mexican, somewhere in her background, and pretty, Phil concluded.

'Philomena, this is Cecily. Where's Mrs Waters?'

'In the kitchen. She's doing lunch.' A touch of liquid accent, the soft caress of Spanish mingled with the drawl of the American South-west. Altogether nice, Phil thought. Her smile was returned four-fold.

'Mrs Waters is our cook, Philomena. You can meet her later. Cecily works the morning shift. Mary comes on from three until seven. Frank is the handyman, and George is the gardener. They'll all be around the house somewhere, after lunch. Why don't you go up to your room and settle in? Cecily?'

The girl nodded and headed for the broad sweep of mahogany stairs that curved gently around to an upstairs landing. There was a painting on the wall, half-way up. A portly pirate, with short black beard, piercing eyes, and a gold watch chain prominently displayed across a half-acre of stomach. It almost seemed there should be an earring in one of his lobes, but of course he wasn't that sort of pirate.

Harry, right behind Phil, with the bags, said, 'The old Boss. He built the place. Been nothin' like him in the family until Penn come along.'

And I can surely believe that, Phil thought. Isn't that the claim—there's a throwback in every family come the third generation? The room to which she was led was almost at the head of the stairs. Cecily threw back the double doors with a touch of grace and stood aside. Harry stopped behind them in the hall. Both waited for Phil's reaction.

'Oh, my,' she murmured as she walked slowly to the centre of the room and looked around. 'Oh, my goodness.' Cecily smiled broadly. The bedroom was four times the size of her own, back home in Rancho Cordova. The walls were pink, the wall-to-wall carpet beige, and the bed covered with a Coat-of-Joseph quilt. Four floor-to-ceiling windows made up one wall, facing west towards the river. The windows stood slightly ajar, inviting her out into the sunshine on the balcony. She resisted. There was too much to be done, too much to be learned.

'I think you've made a mistake,' prim little Philomena said. 'I'm the housekeeper, not the daughter of the house.' But you don't want to change to something else, Phil, her conscience shrieked. Don't be so darn positive!

'No mistake,' Cecily laughed. 'The best room in the house, yes. Mr Wilderman picked it out himself. This one, he said, this one is for Peabody. He calls you that?'

'Yes', Phil laughed. 'But everybody else should call me Phil. You too, Harry.'

'Sure,' the little man said as he swung her bags up on to the bench in front of the dressing-table. 'He hears me call you that and the balloon goes up for sure. Well, maybe when he's not around.'

'The lunch is in twenty minutes,' Cecily offered. 'You want help to unpack?'

'Me?' Phil could just not hold back the giggles. 'I don't have enough in those bags to—well, I don't. But please do stay. I want to ask a question or two.'

Harry took the hint, and left. Phil opened her cases, and transferred the dresses slowly into the huge armoire that took up one corner of the room. It was true, she hadn't brought many clothes. And those she had brought were of two kinds, simple suits for office work, or take-aways from Good Will Industries. At least they looked that way. Cecily watched, somewhat disappointed.

'Tell me about Robbie,' Phil asked. 'Does he go to school? Does he ever see his mother? Is he happy here?'

'Ay Dios mio,' the girl laughed. 'First, yes, he goes to school. But they have vacation. A private school, no? The boy is too sharp. He knows everything. And in his room the computer—you wouldn't believe. He is in trouble once. The police came. Something about tapping into the City's computer system illegally. He—his mother—that is hard to say. His mother has the right to him—you know—the court control. The guardian? But I don't think—especially now that she is remarried—well.' She shrugged a very expressive shoulder. The girl sat down on the corner of the bed. 'It is money, I think. The mother has an income from the Company. The boy also. His mother can't stand to have him around—until she needs money. His money. Then she comes here with much noise and loud argument, you know? And takes him back. Mr Wilderman, he tries now in the court to get permanent control of the child. But the lawyers say you must have family. There must be the home life, and parents. It is a puzzle. There must be action quickly. The court is—ruling? Next week.'

'You mean the case has to be decided as quickly as all that?'

'Yes. I think so. Mr Wilderman, you know, he don't tell us, but we hear. And Mrs Wilderman—well, I don't know. She does not want the boy for love, you understand. She would rather he live with his father. But then she would lose the money. I think—it has been peaceful here for a week. I think something is bound to explode very soon.'

'And Mr Wilderman? He really wants the boy?'

'Of course.'

'For an adopted child he looks very much like Mr Wilderman.'

'But of course. I—oh—the bell. I must serve the lunch. Excuse me—I forgot to say, Welcome.'

'Thank you, Cecily. I'll be down in a minute.'

It took much longer than that. She stopped long enough to scrub herself in the white and gold bathroom, then slipped into one of her better cotton dresses. It was a distinct contrast to her working clothes. A dress warm enough for the mild winter, but sparkling in spring buttercup. Her head was already starting to ache with all she had learned—and had not learned. She pulled out the pins in her hair and unbraided it, setting it straight with a few quick passages of her brush. It made a world of difference to her appearance, but that was something she had failed to notice in the haste of the past ten years.

Fifteen minutes later, she started back down the stairs. Sunlight glittered off the stair-runners and played echo off the little glass squares suspended from the massive chandelier. Behind, on the darker wall, another picture hung. A life-sized oil, it appeared, of a young woman in the spring of her life. She was dressed in a long ball-gown, and was poised looking to her right, a happy smile on her face. Something tugged at Phil's mind. There was something about the picture—but she could not place just what it was. A young woman, with golden hair, smiling at the world! She shrugged her shoulders and went down.

Robbie was waiting for her. 'The dining-room is at the back of the house,' he said. 'When are you going to fix my trousers?'

'Just as soon as we finish lunch,' Phil said casually.

The boy looked at her sceptically, his solemn thin face a mixture of hope and doubt. He stood there for a moment, then turned and walked away down the hall.

Phil was distracted as she followed him. There were more paintings on the walls. Not family pictures, but works of some merit, hung too high for her to read the names of the artists, but not so high that she could not appreciate their excellence. When she turned her attention to where she was going the boy had disappeared. At the end of the hall were a pair of double doors, closed. She was looking down the lateral corridor, wondering where Robbie had gone, when she reached for the knob and went in. Actually she was half-turned, not paying attention to her path. And she smashed into Penn.

His arms came out, almost automatically, and kept her from falling. More than that. They wrapped themselves around her and pulled her in solidly against his vibrant strength. All his actions seemed programmed, not real. He held her close, muttering something she could not make out. She relaxed against him, enjoying the feeling.

One of his hand wandered to her hair, tumbling through it like a leaf in a mill-stream. The other moved to the small of her back and pulled her closer, ever closer. The warmth and comfort of it all had taken her completely by surprise. The hands moved up to cup her head, and his lips brushed across hers gently.

Gently, at first. They came again, insistently, demanding, drawing out of her all the emotions she had stored for twenty-seven years. Stored and never shared. Until now. It was too much of a demand. Her own hands were trapped against his chest. She wriggled them loose and felt them follow the flow of his ribcage, around his back as far as she could reach. And then, as suddenly as the assault had begun, he pushed her back, away from him. 'Who?' he asked bitterly. And all her castle of dreams collapsed.

'Philomena,' she quavered.

'Damn!' He stepped away, widening the gap beyond touch. 'I don't know what came over me,' he sighed. 'I was thinking of something, and there was the smell of your perfume—damnit, Peabody, it reminded me of someone. I'm sorry.'

She had managed to regain her breath by then, and some semblance of her mind. There was a feeling of loss involved—what had tasted so sweet was bitter. But she was determined not to let it show. 'No need to apologise,' she said primly. 'I've been kissed before. To be honest, I rather enjoyed it.'

'That's kind of you,' he chuckled. 'And honest. I like that. But I want you to know I don't run around the house assaulting elderly ladies.' He offered an arm. For himself, she knew, but it felt warmingly good. 'They're about to serve lunch.'

She led him to the table, wrestling all the way with her own thoughts *Elderly lady!* Good lord, he's got *me* thinking that way now. Philomena Peabody, twenty-seven going on fifty! It was nice, that kiss. She *did* enjoy it. She had been kissed by men before—but so long ago she could hardly associate name with face in her memory. And I mustn't let him think—what he's thinking.

'I'm not really *that* old,' she told him. If he wants to pursue the subject, now's the time!

'No, of course not,' he rumbled. 'Sit over here next to me.' He held a chair for her. Phil slipped into it, biting her lip in disgust. He *didn't want* to pursue it—or her, for that matter. Why should that seem important to her? A gong sounded out in the hall. Robbie came in, thumping, in his seven-league boots. Harry was not far behind.

And there's another question answered, Phil thought. Harry eats with the family. So he's not a servant, he's a—what? And Robbie, sitting all hunched up at the far end of the table, looking as if he expected to be poisoned by the cook. His hands were grimy, and there was a streak of something—chocolate?—on his chin. Phil's household soul rebelled. She beckoned to the boy. He looked sullenly, then got up with much reluctance and came around the table to her side. She pulled his head closer so she could whisper in his ear.

'I do the trousers, you wash the hands,' she said. 'And the face too, for that matter.'

The boy considered. He had his father's habit. His head was tilted to one side as he thought, but not an inkling of a smile crossed his face. 'OK,' he said, and thumped out of the room.

'OK?' Penn, looking at her but not seeing, the pads behind his dark glasses still fixed in place. Silence. 'I know it has to do with Robbie. I never realised how noisy he is when he walks. What's going on?'

'He's doing me a favour,' Phil replied. 'We have this bargain going. And all teenagers sound like a herd of buffalo. Even the girls.'

'At least he didn't yell. You're a good influence on that boy, Peabody. You could have been his mother.'

She had her water glass at her lips when he said that, and almost drowned as the fluid went down the wrong pipe. He bent over the corner of the table and patted her back a couple of times. Patted, in his style, Phil thought.

A couple more of those and he'll break my back. *I could be the child's mother?* Robbie is thirteen and I'm twenty-seven. So it's biologically possible, I suppose. But again, that urge to tell him—if he wanted to know. 'Me being Robbie's mother is faintly possible,' she offered with a touch of whimsy in her voice. 'But just barely so. There's this matter of age between us.' And having thrown out the gauntlet for the second time, she relaxed in her chair, waiting to see what he would do.

Cecily came in at that moment with a serving-tray, and set it down in front of him. 'Don't go on about your age, Peabody,' he said firmly. He reached for the carving-knife, and, as Phil held her breath, did an adequate job of carving the roast. And that, she told herself, is the last time I'm going to bring up the subject. When they take the pads off his eyes he'll know better, and I'll be back at my word-processor faster than he can say *who the hell are you*!

She ate more than she had intended. Lunch was usually a sandwich. Mrs Waters was obviously a cook *par excellence*. Phil wandered out to the kitchen for an introduction. The cook was a good advertisement for her wares. Short, well-rounded, flushed cheeks, grey hair. Somebody's mother, looking for a family to love. 'Been here thirty years,' she admitted. 'Mr Waters was the gardener here—before George. But, the war and all, and we never had children, so I stayed. I seen Penn grow up. He was a happy kid—and a happy young man, until his sister died. Since then—well, he's changed. Needs some lovin', that man.'

'His sister died?'

'Boating accident. The pair of them used to race up and down the river in those speedboats and all. Neither one never listened to what nobody had to say. Hit a piece of driftwood, she did. Turned the boat over, broke her neck. She was racing him. He never forgot that. Killed her man too. But he wasn't a Wilderman.' The tone of voice gave to indicate that *therefore the husband didn't count in the scheme of things*.

Robbie came through the swinging doors. 'I washed my hands,' he said. 'And ate all my lunch. Now?'

'Now,' Phil laughed. 'Thank you again, Rose. We'll talk later on. Come on, Robbie.' When the door swung shut behind them Rose Waters stopped what she was doing, put her hands on her hips, and contemplated the back of the door. 'Well,' she said 'I *do* declare. Make a nice housekeeper, that one—make a better wife!'

Not even dreaming of such a fate, Phil and Robbie tumbled up the stairs and into her room. Cecily had resurrected an old pedal Singer sewing-machine from somwhere in the attic, and it stood rather forlornly in the middle of the beige rug. But it worked. 'Up on this chair now, Robbie,' she ordered. The boy, still suspicious, climbed up on the low flat chair and moved as she directed. While she measured and pinned she tried a little conversation.

'When does your school open again, Robbie?'

'Pretty soon.'

'Like it, do you?'

'Ummph.'

With a mouthful of pins Phil could hardly question him at length. 'What do you want to be when you grow up?'

'An adult.'

She looked up quickly, and caught him in a smile. He did his best to erase it, but failed. The grin spread gradually across his face as she made a mark in the air with her finger. 'One for you,' Phil told him. 'But watch yourself, wise guy. Two can pun as easy as one.'

'Well, stupid people keep asking me that,' he returned. The sulky expression was back.

'And that puts me in *my* place,' she chuckled. 'Skin out of those trousers now, and I'll get them sewn.'

'I—I didn't mean you, Miss Peabody,' he defended. 'And I don't take my trousers off when there's girls in the room.'

'Thank you on both counts,' she chuckled. 'But I'm not a girl—I'm a woman.'

'I—I don't think I know what the difference is.'

'I don't think I do either,' Phil returned. 'Scoot out of here now. I'll have all of these ready in about an hour.' The boy managed one more tiny smile, and was gone.

Her first major task of the day finished, Phil decided to wander. She saw Cecily leave, driven off by Frank the handyman in a very plebeian Ford. The sun was bright outside. At the end of February, in the sun, the temperature stood at seventy degrees. It would get colder at sunset. Even worse if clouds settled down from the mountains to the east. There was snow in those mountains, deep snow. Lake Tahoe was under a blizzard, the weatherman had said at midday. And that only a couple of hours away by road. But now it was worth a walk. Phil strolled out on to the veranda, and wandered around to the back of the house.

It was all too confusing, this house, the Wildermans—husband and wife fighting over the boy. Not exactly what you could call a tug-of-love case. Maybe Robbie was right. Maybe they both hated him. But why? He was an adopted child, but he resembled Penn so closely—

could that be the source of the bitterness? And if Mrs Wilderman was intent on getting the boy back, what would she do next? I just hope, Phil told herself, that I'm done and gone from here before the inevitable explosion.

CHAPTER FIVE

THE remainder of the week was a string of little scenes, as Philomena put her hands to organising the household. There was the early morning uproar that brought her up in her bed. It came from behind the connecting door which she had noted but not checked. She slipped into her robe and padded barefoot in the general direction of the problem. The door was unlocked, and on the other side Penn, dressed only in pyjama bottoms, was vainly trying to avoid Harry's ministrations. The bedroom was dim, almost dark.

'I don't want a bath,' Penn said grimly. 'For God's sake, Harry, can't you get the eye drops closer to the eyes?'

'I could if you would stop wigglin' around like a fish on a hook.'

'Oh, so now it's my fault?'

'Look, boss, it's been your fault for two weeks. I hadda refill the prescription four times already. Everybody in the drug store thinks I'm drinking it.'

'Ah. Afraid of your reputation, are you?'

Phil ghosted across the floor. 'Let me do that,' she told Harry. He surrendered the dropper without an argument. 'Sit still. Stop acting like a little baby,' she warned Penn. Harry almost swallowed his tongue, and faded out of the room.

'Baby, is it?' He was a tiger now, all sleek and deadly. She paid his objection about as much attention as she had

71

her sisters' under similar conditions.

'I call it as I see it,' she said firmly. 'Hold still.' Her thumb forced his eyelid up, and two precise drops fell on to his eyeball. 'Is that any better?'

'Lucky,' he grumbled. 'So you got it all. Lucky.'

'You bet,' she chuckled. 'We'll try for two.' Her thumb went out again. He shrugged away, and almost got the digit in his eye. 'I said sit still,' she commanded.

'Yes ma'am.' A very docile comment, that foreshadowed troubles to follow. A tiny grin flicked at the corner of her mouth as she repeated the eyedropper exercise.

'There now, that wasn't too bad, was it?'

'No, Mommy.'

'Don't be a smart-aleck,' she warned.

'Or you'll turn me over your knee? How about a little retribution?' He lunged at her, managing to find one wrist, and pulled her down across his knees. 'Now, Miss Know-It-All, try this one for size.'

It wasn't her time of day, frankly. She did anything better in the afternoon. But there wasn't a great deal of time to object. He had her trapped, pinioned, and crushed up against his naked chest before she could catch her breath. It was about as close as she had ever been to a naked man, and the lack of experience told on her. What followed replaced at least two of her normal three cups of coffee. His lips came down on hers again, softly, gently. His breath smelled like warm clean breezes. *And I haven't even brushed my teeth,* she thought wildly. It didn't bother him. The gentle assault became mental torture. He sealed her off from every outside contact, forcing her to concentrate on him, and him alone. Her nerves filed complaints—rioting complaints. They were ignored. The hand behind her head was no longer needed to lock her in place. She had totally surrendered. And then it was over.

She struggled to sit up. At least it was affecting him also, she noted. He's as out of breath as I am. And something more. That strange expression on his face, as if he had tried something awful and found he liked it!

'Damn it, Peabody,' he muttered. 'You've done it again!'

'Of course,' she returned, as the experience whirled from pleasure to bitterness. 'It's all my fault, right? I took advantage of you.' Her hand reached out against her will, and stroked the curling hair on his massive chest.

'Right,' he grunted. His two hands under her armpits lifted her straight up and set her down on her feet. 'For the sake of my peace of mind, please get the hell out of here!' She fled back into her own bedroom, slammed the connecting door behind her, and frantically fumbled with the key.

It spoiled the whole morning, but the next day, and every day thereafter, he appeared politely at her door, eyedrops in hand. She would lead him over to her bed, sit him down comfortably, and administer his daily dose. And as each day passed, she wished crazily that he might pull her down into his lap again.

With Robbie, things were a little different. The first three days the boy gloomed around the house in his new jeans, disappearing into his room whenever she tried to make conversation. 'Hiding with his computer,' Cecily told her. 'It talks back, but it can't give him any orders.'

On the fourth day she trapped him in a corner and refused to let him go. 'I mean to talk to you, Robbie,' she insisted. 'And if it means that I have to follow you all over the house, even to the bathroom, I'll do it.'

'I'll go in my room and lock the door,' he muttered.

'I've got a key to every room in the house,' she returned, jingling her key-ring at him. He thought about it for a minute or two, and then gave up.

'So talk.'

'Don't you have any friends, Robbie?'

'Not around here. In St Louis, yes. I talk to them through the computer network.'

'Lord, that must make a tremendous telephone bill.'

'He doesn't care so long as it keeps me quiet. Didn't you know that?'

'I know that your father is very worried about you,' Phil snapped. 'Between the lawyers and the court case, he's about to go through the roof. Do you *want* to go back to your mother?'

'No. No, I don't.' The defiance had disappeared. He was just a lonely little boy.

'Then you have to help, Robbie. You have to get out in the sunshine—get a little exercise. How about touring the city with me?'

'Well—I'd rather play with my computer.'

'I'll pull out all the fuses in the house if you don't get outside,' she threatened.

'Why are you so serious about all this? I'm nothing to you.'

'Of course you're something to me. Everybody is something to everybody. Don't they teach you *anything* in that school of yours?'

'No, they don't. I don't understand you. Women are like my mother—and you're not. I think you've got a crush on my—on him!' Those dark eyes bored through her like daggers. She caught her breath.

'That would be a likely way to commit suicide,' she returned, even though her heart wasn't in it. 'Get yourself a jacket while I see if I can rustle up a car.'

'You are funny, Peabody—er—Phil? You rustle cattle, not cars.'.

'Not where I come from, buddy. The clock is running. Scoot.'

Phil's life had been marvellously improved by the reappearance of her car. It arrived three days after her, and seemed to have been—perhaps resurrected would be the best word for it. The engine had been tuned, the brakes re-lined and adjusted, it sported four—no five— new tyres, and the whole rackety thing had been re- painted. The only thing she could object to was the colour. An ancient Japanese car masquerading in Kelly Green was just not her cup of tea. But it ran.

They made their first visitation to Sutter's Fort. Once it had stood on a hill, distant from the confluence of the Sacramento and the American rivers. Now the city had grown up around and past it, its ruins had been reconstructed by the state, and it stood its vigil just a short distance up Capitol Avenue from the State House.

The wall around the fort looked newer than it ever had in Sutter's time. The original wall had been eighteen feet high, made of adobe. The replacement was lower, of painted brick. The central building, the trading post, glowed in a new coat of paint. And the low workshops that stood against the inside of the walls now sold souvenirs. Robbie was impressed but not very. His reaction fell into that gap that Phil defined as 'under- whelmed'.

'Junk,' he commented. 'Tourist stuff. And I read somewhere that John Sutter was a fake.'

'Did you now,' Phil chuckled. 'I thought the jury was still out on that. So maybe he wasn't a Swiss nobleman.

You can't dispute that he established the first white settlement in Northern California, and if it hadn't been for the Gold Rush in 1849 he would have been a very wealthy man.'

'That don't make sense, Phil.' She smiled at him. Her name had come out naturally—and that was a start. 'How could he go broke because of the Gold Rush?'

'It wasn't hard,' she returned. 'Thousands did. But John Sutter had his own way. He wanted to make his money from wheat. There were plenty of customers. Bread cost a fortune in the Gold Rush days.'

'So what was the problem?'

'Wheat has to be planted, tended, and harvested. In the end every labourer that Sutter recruited gave up the agricultural work and went off to pan gold for themselves. Sutter went so far into debt that there was no escape. Want to see some more?'

'Like this?'

'Well, it's hard not to be like this, Robbie. Everything from the old days went to wrack and ruin. It's only been in the last few years that things have been reconstructed. But there's a lot to learn. How about if we go down to Old Sacramento?'

'It's your car,' he grumbled, but she could actually see him relax. So she drove west, skirting the traffic problems on the Capitol Mall, the wide expanse of road that ran from the Capitol building itself down to the river, on the order of the great boulevards of Paris. She also had to dodge the traffic around the K Street Mall, a shopping district that was being overhauled to allow the use of LRV's—light rail vehicles.

They left their car parked in the underground facility in the mall and walked across into the Embarcadero area, the flat plain between Route Five and the river. Reconstruction of the old city was not yet complete, and might never be, but as they walked from block to block they saw it all as it might have been when this little corner of the world was the gateway to the goldfields. There were drapers and drugstores, grocers and hardware, mixed together with saloons, gambling halls, and banks. Not to mention the Hastings building, and the statue which marked the Western terminal of the Pony Express.

'You mean to tell me that they actually lifted the whole town up over fifteen feet?' Robbie's scientific mind found it all improbable.

'More than that in some places,' Phil laughed. 'You know the original city was almost swept away several times in the early days. But instead of just moving away, they dredged the river, lifted all the buildings with hydraulic jacks, and filled in underneath them. And if you think all of that is fairy tales, young man, just run across the street there. You can still look down at the original building, below the present street level.'

Phil stayed where she was and watched as he ran the gauntlet of traffic to have a look. She had had enough. Her feet hurt. If the Bee had suddenly predicted a twenty-foot rise in the river level, Phil was prepared to stand and drown rather than move another step. Robbie walked back slowly.

'Convinced?'

'Yeah. I'm convinced. It's hardly believable though, is it? How could they afford all that?'

'You have to remember that in those days, Robbie, practically all the gold mined in the United States flowed through this city. And a little of it stuck on every hand it passed through. So now, what have you learned?'

He pulled himself up out of his normal slouch. 'I've learned that sightseeing is hard work. My feet hurt.'

Which led them back to the house in a companionable mood, about four o'clock in the afternoon. 'I'm gonna go watch television,' the boy commented. He made himself up a bologna sandwich and a glass of milk, and wandered off.

'Television?' Phil asked. 'I didn't see any antennae on the roof. Have they run the cable out here yet?'

'Nope,' Rose laughed. 'Satellite antenna. Out behind the swimming-pool it is. Gives us one hundred channels twenty-four hours a day, and not a worth-while programme on any of them.'

'But Robbie likes it, I suppose?'

'He sure does. A mite more companionable, the boy is,' Rose commented as she prepared the dinner. 'Roast lamb tonight. Can I give you a hint, Phil?'

'You bet, Rose. Shoot.'

'Maybe you ought to,' the cook muttered. 'Shoot, that is. Find out what Mary is doing.'

'Well, according to the schedule she's supposed to be cleaning the downstairs rooms. Cecily does the upstairs in the morning and serves lunch. Mary does the downstairs in the afternoon and serves dinner. No?'

'That's what the schedule says.'

'I see.' Phil bit her lip. The only thing she hated worse than trouble was letting a little trouble go long enough to become big. 'I'd better go change and clean up,' she said. 'And then I'll see.'

'You bet you will.' Rose was not going to say any more, so Phil got up, stretched, slipped off her shoes and went off, not expecting to find that there was a serpent in the Garden.

The house seemed very still as she made her way up the stairs. *It's like one of those Gothic horror stories,* she told herself as she paused in front of the portrait on the wall. 'You wouldn't haunt me, would you?' she asked the picture. The old pirate seemed to grin back at her. With that reassurance she went, barefoot, up the rest of the stairs.

The door to her room was closed. She could not remember shutting it, and Cecily had long since gone home. So perhaps the wind blew it, she thought, as she pushed her way in. Across the room a figure was bent over the bureau, and all Phil's clothes were lying in disarray on the floor.

'What in the world are you doing!' She was across the room like an avenging angel. This surprising invasion of her own privacy was almost as bad as a physical attack. Sick to her stomach, Phil clutched at the woman's shoulder. It was Mary Treadway, the second maid. A middle-aged thin woman with iron-grey hair, Mary was the sort of person who could easily be someone's spinster aunt. Instead she was the mother of a large family, always in need, always complaining.

'I—I was just cleaning up,' the maid stammered.

'Cleaning up? Here? It looks as if you're *making* a mess, not cleaning one up. And why up here? You know the programme. Your job is to clean downstairs. Cecily takes care of everything up here.'

'I—I must have forgotten.'

'How could you forget? It was only yesterday that I went over the complete list of duties with you!'

'I don't have to listen to any talk like that.' The thin

face was diffused with anger. Real or false, Phil asked herself.

'No, you don't,' she returned quietly. 'You can always quit.'

A flash of alarm came over the woman's face. 'I—I can't do that,' she almost cried. 'I need the money.'

'Then I think you'd better get yourself downstairs and do the work you're assigned.' Phil felt grim, and her voice reflected her feelings. She watched as the older woman hurried out of the door.

And what do you suppose that was all about, she thought? She forgot? Not a chance. It's true she used to clean this room, until I changed the schedule, but forget? Never. So then what? Checking my clothes? To what purpose? Or maybe it's just snooping; an incurable urge to know everything about everybody. If so, all she found out is that I like expensive underwear. How about that?

Still puzzling, Phil stripped off her clothes, took a quick shower, and climbed into her working-clothes. She made a quick tour, as she did every day, of all the rooms on the second floor. They were immaculate, as usual. Cecily was a cheerful and thorough worker. Phil left Penn's room for last. Because it stands next to mine, she told herself. It was as good an excuse as any.

His room was slightly smaller than her own, with none of the frills. Its colour-scheme was bronze and gold. The windows opened up on to the same balcony. His clothes were hung neatly, all in a row, more suits than she wanted to count, but all in what she classified as 'Corporation' colours—navy blue, grey, pinstripes. As with his son, until Phil had worked over the boy's wardrobe, he tended towards formality. And yet, he was not always formal. She had a few glimpses of the man beneath the disguise.

Wonderful glimpses, that left her staggered. She sat down on his bed, and then fell over on to his pillow.

There seemed to be some residual comfort from it all, some warmth. Left over, of course. He had been gone from the house for hours, and the pillow cases had been changed. What *are* you diddling about, she accused herself, and could not find the answer. A wry smile played on her mobile face. *Back to the salt mines, lady!* She laughed at herself as she swung her feet back on to the floor, brushed down the counterpane, and went downstairs.

There was that feeling again, that mood of Gothic doom. She stopped in the bend of the stairs, concentrating this time on the painting of the young woman on the opposite wall. There was some ethereal vagueness about the girl. She looked like someone. *Someone I know!* Again it escaped her, and she went on down.

Robbie was in the game-room at the back of the house, glued to the ten thousandth re-run of a Tarzan movie. A youthful Johnny Weissmuller swung through the vines, chasing after Jane. Phil stayed for a moment. She liked the really old movies, and the dialogue was just right. 'Me Tarzan, you Jane.' What a lovely bunch of writing that was! Chuckling quietly she ruffled Robbie's hair and headed for the door. To her surprise the boy followed her movement, and smiled.

Her tour of inspection swept on, through the dining-room, where there was dust on the sideboard, into the living-room, where the cushions were in some disarray, and out into the hall, hunting Mary. And found her.

The maid was talking to someone on the telephone. Talking softly, swiftly, with her eyes continually sweeping the hall. As soon as she saw Phil appear she downed the telephone and did her best to look industrious. Phil was tired of being the disciplinarian. She swept by Mary without saying a word, and went out into the afternoon sunshine looking for Mr Yu, the gardener. There was something very comforting about sharing the old man's garden—and his dry wit.

Dinner that night was more relaxed than meals had been since she came to this—palace. Penn was in a good mood, allowing her to administer the eyedrops before the meal with not a single quibble. 'Things went well today?' she hazarded.

'They surely did,' he said, 'but I can't carve this darn roast.'

'I'll do it,' she offered. 'You don't have to be totally independent. Not here.'

He tendered her the carving-knife and fork, and a big smile. The last so startled her that she almost dropped the other two. He leaned back in his chair. 'We settled a part of that business out at the Mother Lode,' he said. It was the first time he had ever introduced business into a casual conversation. Two firsts for the day, Phil crowed to herself. Robbie smiled at me, and Penn said a few nice words!

'I never did understand what it was all about,' she tempted.

'You know, of course, that we own a dozen or more small mines in El Dorado county. They were open into the 1930s, but the costs of extracting gold were just booming, so my Grandfather closed them. There's plenty of gold left there, mind you, but it just cost more that it was worth to get it out. The United States government had pegged the price of gold at thirty-five dollars an ounce, and there it stayed. Now, things have changed.

The government no longer tries to control the price of gold. Of course extraction costs have gone up, too. But today, one ounce would cost us about one hundred and sixty dollars to extract—and gold prices are pretty firm in the neighbourhood of three hundred and thirty dollars an ounce. So, it could be profitable.'

'But?'

'Yes, there's a *but*. But the people who live in El Dorado county are suburbanites. They don't want the massive machinery that we would need for open-pit mining. Well, some of them don't. Today we made agreements with three of the towns which allow us to reopen four of the mines, provided we don't go to open-pit mining. I think we can still make a profit. How did your day go?'

'I think I wore out a pair of shoes,' Robbie interjected. Another surprise. To that moment he had never said a word at table. 'She took me sightseeing. I must have walked fifty miles!'

'Poor you,' Phil teased. 'I think it was more like five.'

'But I got even,' the boy returned, grinning. 'I think her feet hurt more than mine did.'

'That must have been a sight to see, all by itself,' his father commented. The two of them launched into a heated discussion about places they had been and admired, leaving Phil sitting in a conversational backwater, happy to hear them making real family talk. Harry was out of it too. She caught him once with a big smile on his face, and he winked at her, as if *she* might be responsible for breaking the log-jam. Which of course I'm not, she told herself regretfully.

At the end of the meal she threw them a bombshell, without meaning to at all. 'Tomorrow is Sunday,' she said as a reminder. 'All the help has the day off, and——'

'All except George Yu,' Penn told her. 'He comes into the house and we eat Chinese for the day.'

'Well, that had me worried,' Phil said. 'I have to go home tomorrow.' A heavy silence fell at the table. All three of the men laid down their utensils and stared at her. 'Did I say something terrible?' she asked.

'Yes,' Robbie returned.

'I think so,' his father added. 'We hadn't expected you to leave us, as if you were hired help.'

'Well, that's what I am,' she returned defensively. 'And besides, it's only for the day. I have to check up on my *own* house, and pick up some more clothes. And my sisters! Sally will be back from her honeymoon, and the other two will want to beat me up, I'm sure.'

'Well, I won't let them,' said Robbie, his face flushed, both fists formed and resting on the table-top.

'I'm just joking,' she hastened to add. 'I don't mean they'll beat me up—I'm older than they are.'

'And they respect your grey hairs,' Penn chuckled.

'She don't have any——'

'That's enough, Robbie. If Philomena needs a day off to go home, we must consider ourselves lucky to have her the rest of the week. What time do you want to go?'

'Early, I suppose,' she said, trying to hide her own groan. 'There's nothing I like about the word early, but I've a lot to do.'

'I'll bet there is,' Penn said. 'By the way, I brought your pay-cheque home.' He handed her an envelope. She tucked it under her plate for the moment, and waited for dessert to be served.

Despite her hatred of things early, she was up and dressed by six-thirty. There was a noise at her door by seven. Penn, wanting his eyedrops administered before she disappeared. 'Just a week and a half more,' he said quietly as she went about the job with dispatch. 'Dr Morgan says everything is coming on fine, provided I just don't rush things. I can see much better.'

'Well, he's right,' she sighed as she applied new pads. 'After all this time it would be silly to take chances. Whatever took you to the Antarctic in the first place?'

'Government secrets,' he chuckled. 'They were looking for coal, so they imported a mining expert.'

'But—coal isn't your line!'

'Hey,' he laughed. 'After ten years in our typing pool and you don't know that Pacific owns open-pit coal mines all over the West?'

'Well, I don't read all that stuff,' she huffed. 'I just type it. Most of you people write as if you had swallowed a dictionary. You need more warmth in your correspondence!'

His hand trapped hers, and his other joined, sliding over the softness at her wrist, and up her forearm. 'Warm, like you,' he muttered. He was looking at something beyond her ken, feeling something more than her arm, dreaming something? It would have been simple for her to pull away. Robbie had come out of his own room and was staring at them. But Phil just did not want to. There was too much pleasure to be had from his hands. Pleasure like nothing she had ever experienced before.

'Well, I won't keep you.' He disengaged her gently, lowering her hand rather than dropping it. 'Have a good day.'

'I will,' she promised softly, and stared after him as he made his way back to his own bedroom, using the wall as a guide. It amazed her how proficient he was. How strong. How gentle. How—'Dear lord, Phil,' she muttered to herself. 'It isn't as if you were going to *eat* him.'

'What did you say?' She turned around, startled. Robbie was still standing there, fully dressed.

'Nothing,' she improvised. 'I was—just clearing my throat.' She managed a dismal hacking cough to illustrate. 'And what brings you out so early, young man?'

'You.' He partnered her as she went down the stairs.

'Your car is out front.' Mr Yu, dressed in slacks and white shirt, held the door for her. 'Frank filled up the tank and checked the oil.'

'Silly,' Phil remarked, but was warmed just the same. After all, she had only driven the car forty miles since the last time Frank had checked it out. She strolled down the stairs. Robbie went right along with her. As she reached for the door handle she looked over at him. I do believe he's growing like a weed, she thought. His eyes are dark grey! Dark, intense eyes.

'And just what are you up to?'

'I'm going with you.'

'Not *may* I go with you?'

'No. Just I'm going. You need somebody to look after you. Dad said last night you are really a *little* thing.'

'I'm not all *that* little.'

'Well, I'm going anyway. You're a girl—a woman. Whatever. Somebody's got to look after you.'

Phil knew when she was beaten, and surrendered gracefully. 'How kind you are.' The boy seemed to swell up just the slightest bit. He ushered her into the driver's seat, closed her door behind her, and went around the car to climb in. As she drove away a peculiar thought hit her.

The boy. Is he going just to keep me company, or to make sure I come back? Is it possible that I mean something to him? As he means something to me? She chewed on the idea all the way out to the house in Rancho Cordova.

'That's an old house,' Robbie said as they drove up into the yard. 'Funny kind of a house to see in the middle of all this.' Phil followed his waving hand. It *did* seem that a dozen more high-rise buildings had come into existence in the short time she had been away.

'It's a farmhouse,' she said as she led the way up to the front door and fumbled for her key. 'When I was a little girl this was all a big farm, and my daddy was a farmer.'

'But it's not now?'

'No,' she said softly. 'My father had no sons—only girls. It takes a great deal of muscle to be a farmer. Muscle and brains. And Dad left so many debts we had to sell the land. But that's last year's news. Come in, Robbie.'

He stepped over the pile of mail lying on the floor behind the mail slot. She stopped to pick it all up. Bills, advertisements, magazine subscriptions—she sorted them all out on the way to the kitchen.

'Now the first thing we do,' she told the boy, 'is open a few windows. The house smells as if it hasn't been lived in for years!' And so the day began. There was dusting to do, some washing—somehow the living-room furniture had accumulated jelly fingerprints—and some laundry to be done. Robbie followed her around like a shadow. It wasn't until midday that Phil got around to the mail. Most of it was disposable. But there were four or five hand-delivered envelopes, with no stamps. She tried the first.

'We're home,' the first note said. Sally. 'I'll have to call her,' Phil told Robbie. 'That's my youngest sister. The baby of the family.'

'How about that,' Robbie returned. 'I'm the oldest *and* the youngest in my family. I wish I had a little sister.'

'It could happen,' she told him absent-mindedly. 'Your Dad's still a young man. He could marry again. Look at this!' Four of the envelopes were identical. 'Call me!' the first one said. 'Call me !!!!' the fourth one said. And the ones in between were the same, but with fewer exclamation marks. 'My sister Samantha,' Phil explained to a giggling Robbie. 'She's impatient.'

'Me too. No lunch way out here?'

'Not much,' she returned. 'A can of spaghetti? I never keep lunch stuff around.'

'I'll take it,' he said enthusiastically.

While he was eating she dialled Sally's new number. The response was electric. 'It's wonderful,' the girl gushed, and then invested ten minutes in the details, concluding with, 'Phil, you've just *got* to get married!'

'And who would have a spinster like me?' Phil returned through the forming tears. 'I've got a mint of work to do before I go back, Sally.'

'You're at home?'

'Yes, for a little while.'

It should have been no surprise, but when the doorbell went at three o'clock, and she opened it to all three of her sisters, Phil was almost in a state of shock. One at a time she could handle—three were just too many. She fell back into the living-room, and all three of them started yelling at her at once. There came a terrible clatter down the back stairs, and Robbie was standing close in front of her, fists half-raised, his face flushed.

'Don't you yell at Philomena,' he roared. They all

stopped, with mouths half opened. After a pregnant moment Samantha said, 'And who in the world is this?'

Phil put both hands on the young man's shoulders. 'This is Robbie,' she said warningly. 'I told you I had found myself a man, didn't I?'

'And you'd better leave her alone,' the boy threatened, 'or I'll get you all.'

'Phil, I just have time,' Deborah interrupted. 'Our trip to Vegas is on, and I can bring the girls over here in no time. We'll be back on Wednesday.'

'I hope you don't,' Phil said firmly. 'I won't be here. Robbie and I are leaving in about twenty minutes——'

'And she's never coming back,' the boy threatened. Debbie managed an impatient laugh.

'Come on, Phil, the joke's over,' she grated. 'Let's get life back to normal in this family.'

'And Phil,' Samantha interrupted. 'Albert and I have just got to talk to you about the terms of the Trust. He—I—want enough money to open a new office in a better district, and——'

'Sally,' Phil ordered. 'Take Robbie out in the kitchen, will you.' She watched as her baby sister complied. 'Now, you two. Things have changed around here. I don't *want* to go back to the old ways. I have my own life to lead, and it doesn't include baby-sitting, or trying to break the terms of Daddy's will. You two tear at my heart. You know Mother told me to take care of you. I've done a terrible job. I don't know when I've met two more selfish people in my life.'

She stopped to stab at a tear forming in her eye. 'Now you both have families to look after, and jobs to do. Just go and do them. When I get back on an even keel I'll contact you. But don't hold out any wild hopes. Things have changed permanently.'

The two of them stared at her for a moment, and then picked up their bags and left. Moments later Sally came out of the kitchen. 'Atta girl,' she said softly, kissing Phil on the cheek. 'You should have done that years ago. You know what Charley and I want from you?'

Phil's tears were really rolling now. She looked at the blur that was her youngest sister and waited. 'What *we* want is to love you.' And with that Sally was gone too. Robbie came out of the kitchen.

'You forgot this,' he said, waving another envelope at her. She managed to dry up the storm, and tore open the plain white envelope. Inside was a cheque, made out in her name, for four times her usual salary. The tears started again. She dropped into the armchair and let them flow. Robbie came around in front of her, with both hands in his pockets.

'What's the matter now?' he asked patiently.

'I don't know,' she admitted. 'I just don't know.'

'Girls are funny,' he said conclusively. 'Let's go home now.'

CHAPTER SIX

PHILOMENA devoted the drive back to the city to deep thought. Robbie climbed into the car without a word, his face relapsing into his typical teenage scowl. The inbound traffic was light because it was Sunday afternoon, but they were still serenaded by the city-dwellers' bird-song—the whiz and hum of tyres as cars passed, the rattle of gratings as heavy vehicles hit the overpasses at speed, the blinking of headlights as fools tried to exceed the fifty-five-miles-an-hour speed limit, and the occasional blasting wail of a horn as one bad driver signalled curses at another.

It was all background. Phil had her own problem. She went back over all that was said between sisters, and still believed herself to be right—but at a painful cost. Little sisters don't become spoiled by themselves, she told herself fiercely. It takes two to tango. They are what I made them. And now, having laid down the law to my own, I'm darned if I'm not running off to somebody else's family, all set to take up the burden again! And how big a fool does that make me?

Harry waited for them at the bottom step. He opened her door. Robbie made some sort of grunting noise that might, under the wildest circumstances, be interpreted as a 'Thank you,' and then scrambled out of the car. Phil required a great deal more care. Before she left the house she had changed into one of her best dresses, a light wool that matched each of her curves gently, and clung just above the knees. Which made scrambling out of tiny cars something of an adventure. Harry tried to act as if he hadn't noticed the large amount of thigh on display. She tendered him a wry smile, and went up the stairs ahead of him.

It had been a long hard day, and Penn was not quite able to assemble it all. A day set aside out of the rush of time. The sort of splendid day that could be spent outdoors, in the heated pool—damn those eye pads—or just piddling around and listening as George Yu commented on the world, the planets, and the Raiders. Until they had insulted half the world by moving to Los Angeles, the Oakland Raiders football team had been the old man's pride and joy.

But there had been no relaxation in it all today. Mr Yu seemed grumpy. Something about his camellias, and the up-coming flower festival. Something too about how quiet the house seemed without Miss Peabody in residence. And just hearing it said had startled Penn into breaking away and stomping off into the house. 'Bad enough, for God's sake,' he muttered as he fumbled his way into the lounge, 'to be thinking stupid things like that myself, without hearing everybody else in the house come down with a terminal case of Peabody.' He splashed what he thought was Scotch into a tumbler, discovered it was Bourbon, and sipped at it anyway. The whole picture bothered him. Her reaction to Robbie, and to himself, and—his reaction to her. Damn, it bothered him.

Along about four o'clock in the afternoon Harry found him, slumped down in the old Morris Chair in the front sitting-room, still nursing the same glass of Bourbon, down more in spirit than in spirits.

'Ain't nobody set in here since the old man died,' Harry commented softly.

'I know.' There was a time of silence, punctuated by the clink of ice in Penn's glass. 'Have something, Harry?'

'Not me. You know what the doctor said.'

'Yeah, I remember. No wine, no women, and not much song?'

'That about covers it. Funny feeling around the house today.'

'No, don't *you* start that. That's all I've heard all day from George Yu.'

'Crazy Chinaman.' A soft comment, not a criticism, but more like the underlining of a long-held pleasantry.

'Like a fox, Harry. He could have been a stockholder in Pacific Mines and Metal, but he didn't want it. Too much responsibility, he said. I remember him arguing with my father about that. Responsibility brings ambition, ambition brings worry, and—I forget the rest of it. Some Chinese philosopher before Confucius' time. Where the hell is she?'

'Who?'

The glass in Penn's hand seemed to crumble, spreading shards all over the carpet. His reflex action knocked over the bottle of Bourbon at his elbow. It fell to the carpet beside the glass, dumping its contents over his coat sleeve and trouser leg. 'Damn!' Harry moved rapidly over to his side and picked up the flaccid hand.

'Just a nick,' he reported. 'Needs a plaster. What's bugging you? The hearing?'

'Among other things. Next Thursday, Harry, and it's going to be one tough struggle. These bandages don't come off until three days later. I'll walk into that courtroom, the Juvenile judge will take one look at me, and everything goes down the drain. All I've got going for me is character witnesses and past history. Nobody in their right mind would give custody of a child to a blind man. What I need is—damn it, Harry, if I had my sight it would be no problem at all. I'm sure of that! But——'

'But what?'

'Her. What do you think, Harry?'

'I wish I knew what the hell you're talking about, Penn'

'Peabody, damn it. Philomena. What do you think?'

'Nice lady. The kid don't let on, but he likes her. Nice shape. Built classy, not one of these skinny broads. Always used to hate those skinny ones. Every time you try to hug one you get splinters. Not this girl.'

'She's hardly a girl, Harry. And that's the problem. What about the age difference between us?'

'Oh, I don't know, boss. It's hard to tell with a good-looking broad. I'd say there can't be more than eight or ten years between you both. Nothing to worry about. Hardly anybody would notice, these days. Just what are you thinking about?'

'I'm thinking—you'd better find me another glass. And put Scotch in it. I can't seem to find the Scotch bottle.'

'OK, if that's what you want, but that's her car coming up the drive now, and you——'

'And I stink of Bourbon. Good lord. Get this coat off me. Do I have anything right here?'

'That smoking-jacket thing—the one you swore you'd never wear because——'

'Never mind what I swore I'd never—give me the damn thing and get out there and make her welcome!'

All of which brought Harry to the front door all in good

time, and left Penn to fumble around madly trying to rid himself of the Bourbon smell, and at the same time stuff himself into the scarlet smoking-jacket his former wife had given him. The jacket clung, and so did the smell. Draconian measures, he told himself, as he poured the carafe of water over his trouser leg. Better water-wet than Bourbon-wet. It had suddenly become important to make a good impression on a certain lady.

Phil looked back towards Harry as she moved up the stairs. 'You're sure it's OK to leave my old car parked in front of the house?' she asked. There wasn't time for an answer. Moving faster than usual, for some reason she still did not fathom, she cannoned off the solid steel of Penn's chest, rattled around a time to two, and was finally rescued by those arms. For a second she was about to relax, to let it all happen. But then he seemed to pull her closer, to bury her nose against the soft suede of his smoking-jacket. And the smell hit her.

'My lord,' she muttered, wriggling furiously until his surprised arms unfolded and turned her loose. 'Drunk by Sunday evening?' It was hard to hide the disgust in her voice. Drunks and smokers were her favourite hates, and she had no plans for staying close to either category.

'No, I am not,' he returned indignantly. 'I've had one drink today, and managed to spill it all over myself. And just supposing I were? Who are you to—dammit!' She could see him try to suppress his words. His angry throat seemed to choke up in sympathy with his swollen angry cheeks. It was a momentous struggle. She watched, spellbound, having never seen an autocratic man swallow his own words. Her moment of anger had passed. But perhaps the chuckle was a mistake. His hands seemed to find her by radar and fastened on her shoulders, holding her stiffly at arms' length.

'Funny, Peabody?' he asked warningly.

'Er—no, of course not.' After all, he was the boss. She had never held a doubt about that. 'I—I think you must have spilled something,' she offered tentatively, a sort of good-will gesture. It was amazing how quickly he snapped up the olive-branch.

'Yes,' he returned gently. The hold on her shoulders became a gentle squeeze, and then a tentative caress. 'We've missed you, it seems.'

There was nothing she could think of to say. Especially when he leaned forward on a straight line, kissed the fringe of her hair, then corrected his aim and lightly touched her lips. 'Dinner's ready,' he grinned. 'Won ton soup and Mandarin chicken. Mr Yu's been worrying about it all day.'

It was the grin that undid all her resolves. So he smelled like the Jim Beam Distillery—that lopsided little grin took years off his age, charmed her prejudices, soothed her worries—and gave her something to say. 'Great,' she enthused. 'I'm sick of my own cooking! Give me ten minutes to freshen up.'

'Better make that twenty,' he chuckled. 'I need to do some freshening myself.'

'We're going in the same direction,' she chuckled, taking his arm, 'so why don't we share a stair?'

'Poetry?' he groaned, but followed her lead into the house and up the stairs. From the kitchen she could hear a great banging of pans, and a few delectable Chinese phrases that required no translation. As usual, her eye was caught by the haunting painting on the opposite wall. The girl-woman's eyes seemed to follow Phil as she came to a gradual stop. The artist had caught an expression—was it happiness—congratulations? Almost it seemed as if the girl in the painting were at least wishing her well.

'What is it?' he asked, tugging at her arm.

'The painting. The girl——' She struggled for words and found none. His massive head swung in the direction she was looking. It almost seemed that she could see tears beneath the eye-pads, but that was ridiculous. Phil started them up the stairs again. 'It's just that the—she——'

'Robin,' he said in a low tired voice. 'Her name was Robin.'

'Was?'

'Yes.' A blunt word, that cut off the conversation. She escorted him to his door, then returned to her own room. A quick brush-up, that was all she wanted. A quick wash, a struggle with comb and brush through her long curly hair, the briefest of touches from her lipstick, and a knock on the connecting door. Startled, she walked over to it. In all her time in the house she had never thought to lock the connecting door into his bedroom.

'More drops in your eyes?' she asked as he came in.

'Well—it wouldn't hurt, I suppose.' It was the first non-positive statement she had ever heard him make. He was a man who made up his mind quickly, and spoke it immediately. And now, 'I suppose,'—as if there were other objectives to be reached.

'Sit here on the edge of my bed.' She guided him around the furniture. He dropped down, and the old four-poster seemed to groan at the weight. Phil smiled at the thoughts that ran through her brain. He couldn't see, so there was no need to hide the hungry look in her eyes. And he couldn't read minds—she hoped.

Phil feasted on him for a moment, then went over to her own dressing-table where she kept eye-droppers and his prescription. On the way she detoured by the windows and drew the curtains, darkening the room. The dosage was as usual, but her hand shook just the slightest amount.

'Lost your nerve, doctor?' he chuckled.

'It does seem so,' she returned ruefully as she re-loaded the dropper. Make conversation, her mind demanded. But it was hard. He was beginning to have an effect on her that puzzled her. 'I had a little squabble with my sisters,' she offered as an explanation. 'Well, with two out of three. Don't blink, for goodness' sake.'

'Well, don't stick your thumb in my eyeball,' he snapped. 'Two out of three? That's not bad at all.'

'Shows you what a really terrible mother I turned out to be,' she quipped, turning his head so that she could get at the other eye. 'I raised two adult delinquents. This darn pad is sticking to your eyebrow. Whoever put it on this morning wasn't too careful. That didn't hurt, did it?'

'Of course it did,' he laughed. 'You tore off half my eyebrow there, lady.'

'Just not my day,' Phil mourned. 'Hold still, for goodness' sake! You're worse than a basket of kittens!'

'Nobody's ever told me *that* before,' he said as she returned the medications to their proper place. 'Come sit by me, Phil. There's something I need to say to you.'

Her skirt rustled as she complied. The bed complained. 'I'm not sure this bed was made for two,' she teased. Her thumb ran over the edge of his eyebrow, smoothing down the hairs. 'I didn't really pull any hairs out at all,' she mused, accusingly. 'You made that up. Can you see any better today?'

'If you've got all the lights on I'm losing ground,' he said.

'They're not,' she laughed. 'I don't have a single light on, and the curtains are drawn.'

'In that case I'm making marvellous progress. Monday week, that's when the doctors promise the great unveiling.'

'A week from Monday?'

'That's what I said—Monday week.'

'Stop wriggling, or this pad will have the rest of your eyebrow,' she threatened. Her fingers gently smoothed the pad in place, and then, for luck, she kissed the tip of his nose. He reached out for her, but she dodged, giggling.

'I'm not your fourth sister,' he said darkly.

'Oh, do I ever know that,' she sighed. He waited for an explanation—which she had no intention of giving. Why confess to this—this arrogant man—how much he had come to mean to her? She longed for the privilege to brush the hank of hair out of his eyes, to kiss each of his damaged eyes, to—and of course, that was the problem. When the day came to remove those pads, the day when he was fully restored to the light of the world he ruled, Philomena Peabody would become just one of the dull shadows in his life. Someone unnoticed until needed, and then in an absent-minded way. And then what will I do, she asked herself. Go back to my sisters and apologise?

'What are you thinking about?' Again that gentle fumbling sound, as if he had a point and hadn't the courage to come to it.

'Oh, nothing,' she sighed. 'My sister Sally, Won ton soup, Robbie's next protest march—I don't know.'

'Sit down here again.' He patted the bed beside him.

She sank down gracefully, closer than before, and tucked her legs up under her.

'I have a problem with Robert,' he said. 'A legal problem.'

'Yes, I know.' Almost unconsciously she captured his hand and moved it to her lap, between her own warm sympathetic fingers.

'There aren't any secrets in the world?' he asked.

'Not in the kitchen.'

His fingers squeezed hers gently. 'I don't get rid of my blinders until Monday next,' he repeated softly, as if re-telling an old story. 'The Juvenile Court hearing is scheduled for this Thursday.'

'Yes?'

'If I go into court on Thursday I've two strikes against me. First, I can't see; secondly, I don't have a real home for Robert. God, who could believe it would all end up this way?'

'You might as well be honest,' Phil added quietly. 'You've three strikes against you already.' He sat up, rigidly, waiting. 'Robbie thinks you hate him.'

'Oh God, not that too,' he muttered. 'You know this?'

'He told me. He thinks both of you hate him. Both of you.'

'He tells you lots of things?'

'Whoa up,' Phil chuckled. 'It's not that way. He's a crazy upset adolescent. He doesn't like me any more than any of the rest of you—he just sort of—hates me less.'

'But you do get along with him. And that's more than I can do.'

'Or his mother either?'

'I told you once before. His mother's dead.'

'Yes, well, that's more confusion than I want to know

about—please don't explain anything more to me about it. What did you really want to talk to me about?'

'I——' He coughed to clear his throat—or his mind. It was hard to tell which. 'I'd like to hire you for another job, Philomena.'

'I——' A sudden fear clouded her mind. 'I'm only a typist,' she moaned. 'I—what other job?'

'I want that boy.' His hands snatched at hers to emphasise. Her little whimper brought him back to reality. 'I'm sorry,' he said bitterly. 'That's all I seem to do—hurt the people closest to me.' And then it all came out, in a machine-gun burst of words, without pause for breath.

'My only hope is to walk into that court on Thursday with a capable, happy wife on my arm, and a son willing enough to go along with the gag. My only hope. By Thursday morning I've got to be married. That's a pretty hard thing for a temporary blind man to do when he's been away for a long time, has no available choices, and no time to ponder about it. I need somebody who will act the part, is on the scene.' He paused for a moment, his head cocked to one side as if waiting for some comment. She offered nothing. He took a deep breath and continued. 'Somebody who—er—is willing to accept the temporary nature of the whole affair, and that's why I want you to marry me, Philomena.'

She took a deep breath to match his own. 'You want me to——?'

'Marry me. On Tuesday, if I can arrange it.'

Well, she sighed to herself, at least he didn't call me 'Peabody'. That's one step in my favour!

'Well?'

'I'm thinking,' she blurted out angrily. 'Surely you

don't expect a girl to hear something like that and promptly fall at your feet in rapture? I'm thinking.'

'I'll wait.'

'Don't be *that* darn patient,' she snapped. 'I don't expect to get through thinking about it in the next thirty minutes. Why don't you go downstairs and have your meal. I can hear Harry coming up to look for you.'

'We'll both go.' He stood up. The bed creaked in relief. He tugged at her hand, but she refused to budge.

'Go ahead,' she sighed. 'I'm suddenly not hungry any more.'

'But you are thinking about it?'

'I am. But—from where I sit it's all for Robbie, and I have to talk to him first.'

'It's not *all* for Robert,' he returned. 'I'll see you right in all this, Philomena. I—I seem to like you very much. When I get my bandages off, I'll fix things for you. You'll never have to work again, believe me.'

'Ha!' she snorted. 'You think being a mother to Robbie Wilderman is some sort of lead-pipe cinch. And with *you* thrown into the bargain besides?'

'I swear there will be proper compensation for it all,' he said. There it was, that pompous 'I am the head man' tone again.

'Yes,' she snapped. 'I'm sure there will be, and it's only temporary, and now before you really make me angry, go get your supper.'

He mumbled something about 'women' under his breath as he stumbled towards the door. She made not a move to help him, but Harry was just outside, in the hall, and rescued him. Phil sat where he had left her, and tried to think it all out.

Men! He hadn't even attempted to put icing on the

cake. He just set it out there in front of her and dared her to accept. Marry me and save Robbie. A most objectionable man, with a most objectionable son. Good lord, am I some sort of masochist? I've put up with a decade of playing mother—and didn't do too good a job at it, either. And now I'm supposed to dive into a worse mess. How long is temporary? What happens when he takes those darn pads off his eyes and really sees me? And having learned to survive through adolescent sisters, is any of that experience transferable to a sulky-boy type? Oh lord.

She sat there for more than an hour, knowing all along that there was something she had not entered into the equation. It had something to do with *him*—and every time she approached the subject her mind shied away from it like a nervous mare! Finally, about seven o'clock, she gave up the argument and went to do the one thing she knew had to be done.

Robbie's room was just a few doors down from her own. A stereo system was blasting at high intensity from within. Although all the walls were thick, almost sound-proofed, this penetrated. Phil shrugged her shoulders. Only four years ago Sally had been swept up into hard rock—heavy metal as it was known as on the street. She knocked on the door without response, gave it a moment or two, and then barged in. Robbie was sitting at his computer table, hard at work on some word-game. The stereo blasted away from a desk beside him. His right foot was tapping on the rug matching the primitive rhythm of the music. His unruly hair looked as if it had been exposed to perhaps ten seconds' worth of shower. He was wearing a blue pyjama top and his favourite jeans. When she leaned over his shoulder and flipped the stereo off he jumped.

'Hey,' he yelled, and then stopped in mid-sentence when he recognised her. He dropped back into the chair again, and went on punching keys on the computer board.

'I need to talk to you, Robbie,' she said softly. That sullen look swept over his face. He refused to turn around. Phil looked around for the power switch, and shut it down. The computer rumbled a couple of times, its internal blowers slowed to a stop, and quiet reigned. He turned around. A swivel chair, she noted. A poor under-deprived kid.

'Now I've lost the entire computer program,' he growled, but avoided her eyes.

'You'll think of it again some day,' she said very complacently. 'I have some questions, and I need some straight answers. Listen up.' The last two words had a snap to them that brought him up to the mark. It works on boys too, Phil noted, with some pleasure. Maybe I learned how to be a mother after all!

'So?' A touch of insolence, but overlaid by curiosity, and curiosity was winning. Phil looked around. There were four chairs in the room, all loaded with clothes, books, videotapes, and what-have-you. She picked the nearest, dumped its computer magazines on the foor, and sat down.

'Hey,' he protested again. Her eyes roamed around the dishevelled room. He had the grace to blush. 'So it's not neat,' he grumbled. 'I can't have those *women* coming in here every day and getting everything out of order.'

'You sound like your father,' she commented softly, showing just enough steel in her voice so that he knew it was there. 'Starting tomorrow you pick up in here, or

Cecily will, or *I* will.' He got the message. If Phil had to come in and clear things, shortly thereafter there would be hell to pay.

'Is that all you came for?' he grumbled. 'Breaking up my program just about that?'

'No,' she said, showing more steel. The boy was becoming agitated. He moved back into his swivel chair as if to re-establish his position. She didn't give him the time he needed.

'Your father,' she said. 'For some reason he likes you.'

'No, he doesn't,' the boy returned bitterly.

'He does,' Phil continued relentlessly. 'He told me so. I don't know why he would. You're a real cactus.'

Robbie's head snapped up. 'What's that mean?' he demanded fiercely.

'Well, look at you,' she continued. 'When you love people you want to hug and kiss them once in a while. Look at you. You're just like a cactus, loaded with spines and prickles. Some hugger you'd make! Let me tell you something, Robbie. The world is full of people who don't want to be loved—so nobody loves them. You have to give a little to get a little.'

The boy turned all this over in his mind. She could see the gears creaking. 'My father likes me?'

'Of course he likes you. Why do you think he's going through this fire-drill with the court?'

'Because he needs the money,' the answer came.

Phil stifled a giggle. You can be hard with adolescents. You can be direct. You can be bitter. But you can't laugh at them. 'Your father's got enough money to buy out the US Treasury,' she commented. 'And maybe a couple of other countries to go with it. He *wants* you. I don't know why. Do you?'

'Yes,' he returned after a pause. 'I think I do. I haven't been hugged since—since a long time. I suppose that's something you have to put up with when you have women around the house?'

'I suppose so. And you've got a problem, Robbie.'

He watched expectantly.

'Your mother wants to keep you, and she has a new husband. You like him?'

'I can't stand him,' the boy returned. 'He doesn't like to go fishing or swimming or anything. And he don't know a thing about computers. Can you imagine that?'

'Yes,' Phil returned. 'I can imagine that. So you don't like your mother's new husband, and——'

'She's not my mother,' he interrupted bitterly.

'Ah. I had forgotten.' Another moment of silence. 'Did you know that your Dad is planning to get married again?'

The little head snapped around. 'To a woman?'

'Well, that's the usual thing.'

'No, I didn't know.' There was a look of appeal in his eyes. 'I know I won't like her.'

'Well, that *is* too bad.' Phil got up, brushed down her dress, and moved toward the door. 'I thought you and I might become—well, perhaps not friends, but——'

'You mean he wants to marry *you*, Phil?'

'Is that so bad? So I'm not a movie queen. Yes, he wants to marry me.'

'I—and are you going to?'

'I don't know, Robbie,' she told him bluntly. 'It all depends on you. If it's going to start a revolution, then no, I won't marry him. If you and I could live peacefully together, why I thought I might give it a try. What do you think?'

The boy was up from his chair, moving towards her. Awkwardly, but with a hint of his father's feline grace. Thirteen, and he was already an inch taller than she. Much taller, if she slipped out of her two-inch heels. She did just that.

It was just the right touch. Suddenly towering over her, bigger, she could see his face lighten as he came closer. The dominant male, she giggled to herself. At all ages. Now what?

He took her by the hand. 'I want to show you something,' he said. She followed him out into the hall and down towards the stairs. George Yu stood at the bottom.

'You don't eat?' he called up to them. 'Neither of you to eat, and the boss all grumpy. You two come down to the kitchen. I got left-overs. The soup is still hot.'

Phil stopped at the head of the stairs. Robbie looked down and actually smiled at her. His tugging hand led her half-way down, and stopped at the bend.

'There.' He pointed across to where the painting of the woman was half hidden in the shadows.

'There? I like that painting very much. Who is it?'

'That's—that's my mother.' There was a catch in his voice, as if he had some trouble with his throat. Phil dropped to the stair and pulled him down beside her. They both stared at the painting through the interstices of the banister.

'So that's your mother,' she sighed. 'There's something about her—the picture—that's bothered me for two weeks. Something familiar—but I know I've never seen her.'

'Me neither,' the boy returned. 'She died when I was one year old.'

'So long ago,' Phil sighed. 'And you've never been hugged since then, I'll bet.'

The boy cleared his throat, and relaxed his stiffened back. 'No,' he whispered, 'I guess not.' It must have been an unconscious movement. He slid over on the stair until he was touching her, and then suddenly he collapsed in a heap, tears streaming down his face, his head close on Phil's shoulder. Her arms went around him, comforting. She murmured consolation in his ear, and he cried it all out, there on the stairs.

The storm went on for minutes, then gradually decreased to a hiccup, and blew its way out. He fumbled for a handkerchief to wipe his eyes. Dirty, Phil noticed, as any good housekeeper would. He coughed a couple of times, and cleared his throat.

'You didn't get any prickles,' he said, 'so I can't be a real cactus.'

'I guess you can't be,' Phil said in pseudo-amazement. 'Could I have been wrong? I was wrong once before—let me see now—that would have been eighteen years ago.' He managed a chuckle. She flowed gracefully up to her feet and pulled him with her. He wrapped both arms around her, and pulled her close, her soft cheek against his, for comfort.

'I still don't see why that picture bothers me,' she repeated a moment later.

He released her, laughing. 'It's because you look just like her, Phil, didn't you know?'

'I like this hugging business,' she returned. 'How could she look just like me?'

'Well, maybe not *just*,' he said, 'but kind of—well, you know!'

'I'll have to take your word for it,' she giggled. 'And

now I'm really hungry. Why don't we both sneak down to the kitchen and try some of the left-overs?'

'And what are you going to tell my father?'

She was all solemnity again. 'What *should* I tell him?'

'I think—I don't know. I suppose you might make a nice mother for some kid. I don't need one myself, but you'd make a great mother.'

'But not for you,' she probed. That stubborn, sullen look flashed across his face. 'Well, at least have a little sympathy for my elderly bones,' she sighed. 'Take me to your kitchen and feed me—before I have to decide what to tell your father. You won't advise me?'

'Nope.' He went over to the table and sat down, burying his face behind a huge soup spoon. Phil stood in the kitchen doorway, both hands on her hips. Well, I *almost* got you. And there's always a next time, kiddo. She had already decided what she was going to say to Penn.

CHAPTER SEVEN

WHAT with one thing and another, it was late evening before Phil tracked Penn down. The warmth of the sun still lingered. He was lounging out behind the house on a comfortable swing-sofa, with no one else around. She stopped on the edge of the grass to absorb the picture of him. He was leaning back in the swing, both feet planted firmly on the cement that surrounded the pool. His sports shirt was unbuttoned, his raven hair flopped to one side, and worn jeans clung to his supple hips. There was a little frown tugging at his mouth. Altogether too handsome, she told herself. The fingers of his right hand came up and tugged at the pads that covered his eye.

'No!' The half-scream was involuntary. She dashed across to where he sat. 'Don't do that!' she ordered.

'Don't do what?' He was laughing, and that boyish look was on his half-tilted face.

'Don't touch those pads,' she gruffed, doing her best to swallow her fears. 'It's just a week to go. If you take those pads off out here in the bright sun you'll——you'll——'

'I'll what?'

'Don't tease me,' she muttered. 'You know darn well I don't know what would happen. I'm not a doctor or a nurse. But I'm sure you'll——'

'But you're sure I'll do something wrong?' Definite laughter. The frown was gone. And then he gave her a set-down. 'I don't remember any of my employees who worry about me the way you do, Peabody.'

One of his employees, that's the way he thinks of me. So much for all those lovely dreams last night! She stood silently beside the swing, her hands twisting nervously behind her back.

'So you came to tell me something.'

'I came to tell you—I—I talked with Robbie about—about—what you said.'

'So it all depends on Robbie, does it?'

'Well, doesn't it? That's what you told me in the first place!' He reached out a hand in her general direction. Without even thinking, she put her own in his. He tugged at her gently, until she settled down into the swing, as far from him as she could get.

'I put it all very badly, didn't I?' he said softly.

'Yes, you did,' she returned grimly. His hand still held hers, and it disturbed her in some way which she couldn't comprehend.

'I'm not much for speech-making, Philomena. It wasn't *all* for Robbie. Some of it was for me. I need a wife, need one very badly.'

'And that's what you'll get if you make blind choices,' she snapped. 'You'll get one very badly.'

'Low blow,' he returned gravely. 'Blind choices? Semantics, Peabody, or do you mean it?'

'I—I'm sorry. I wasn't thinking. I—'

'Just blurted it all out?'

'Yes.' She had composed herself by this time. Both his hands were on her one, toying with it. 'I'm sorry. You were saying?'

'I was saying I need a wife, Philomena. A woman like you. I happen to like you very much.'

And that, she told herself, sounds about as exciting as a peanut butter sandwich. But it was better than nothing, wasn't it? Because I—I like him very much too. Her resolve returned. She added her other hand to the pile. 'I came out to tell you that if you still want it, I'll marry you—Penn.'

'Ah.' There was a whole host of satisfaction in his one word. He slid over on the swing, agitating it as he moved, until he was sitting hard up against her. *Which was just the way she wanted it*. His hard thigh crushed up against her, his warm arm around her shoulders, gently squeezing. She used her free hand to snatch at the sofa arm as the swing jerked and bounced. Her feet no longer reached the ground, but for some stupid reason her heart was as high as the clouds that temporarily brushed across the sun.

'So now we're engaged?'

'I—I guess so.'

'Good. Now where the—where did I put that thing?' His struggle to get a hand into his pocket without moving away from her was agitating her—not the swing. His elbow kept brushing against her breast, sending shivers up her spine. 'Ah!' The hand came out of his pocket with a small box. He snapped it open with one hand, and held it out to her.

She stared at the diamond ring, stunned, not knowing what to say. It was a small but perfect diamond, set in a circlet of sparkling diamond chips, the whole gleaming on a platinum ring.

'This is where the heroine says *For me*?' she managed.

'That's the line,' he chuckled. 'See a lot of movies, do you?'

'No.' She had finally managed to clamp down on her emotions, and her usually cheerful spirit was leaking through. 'No,' she repeated, 'but I read a great many books. What do I——'

'Now you don't do anything,' he said. His strong tactile fingers snatched the ring from its nest and held it out towards her. Wordlessly she extended her left hand. He fumbled for the right finger, found it, and slipped the ring on.

'It just fits,' she reported, astonished.

'Of course,' he chuckled.

There, she told herself. Of course it wouldn't dare not fit. Not if Penn ordered it! But instead of that surge of anger that had teased her for weeks in such situations, this time she felt marvellously better—happier.

'It's lovely,' she managed to breathe.

'Of course,' he commented.

'Did you ever think that if you keep talking like that somebody might just—hit you?'

'Somebody will, I'm sure,' he agreed. 'But not you, Peabody.'

'No,' she sighed, giving up the war after one battle. 'Not me, I guess. Were you *that* sure of me?'

His arm was around her shoulders again, tucking itself under her left arm, with the tips of his fingers just inches from her breast. She leaned over against him, resting her head under his chin. 'Sure of you?' he said. 'I don't believe I've taken such a risk in many a day.' She started to raise her head. 'No,' he ordered, 'don't move.' She dropped back, sighing. It was pleasant to be coddled. His free arm came across her, resting on her stomach, hand clutching at her hip.

'You're a great deal of woman, Philomena,' he whispered into her hair. 'A great deal of delightfully designed woman. We'll make a good pair, you and I.'

Surely we will, she told herself fiercely. Until my

option runs out, we'll make a great team. And after that—well, I won't think about that. Not right now. She snuggled closer, pulling her legs up under her. He used one foot to start the swing rocking gently. Somehow or other his right hand had moved from her hip and was cupping her breast, weighing it. The pleasure of it all overcame her reluctance, but only for a moment. When her hand moved his away from her breast back down to her waist he sighed deeply.

'Not accustomed to giving samples?' he asked. There was something wrong with his voice. It sounded as if some—passion—were choking him, fighting him. 'Not even for your fiancé?'

'How could I know?' she answered, her own voice husky with strain. 'I've never been engaged before. Perhaps I just don't know the drill?'

They rocked back and forth for minutes. Her muscles relaxed as the tension faded. She lay against him, savouring the warmth, wondering whether she should have—but the chance had passed.

From out of the mist of her day-dreams his voice finally penetrated. 'And then on Tuesday we can be married,' he was saying. 'Judge Caldwell will do it for us in Chambers, I'm sure. Then comes the hearing, followed by a short honeymoon at home. I'll send Robbie off with Harry, and give the others a vacation.'

And that, she told herself, puts a period to all the dreams. Orange blossoms and a long white gown, and music—'Here comes the bride—'All down the drain. She nestled closer to him, and hid her face against his shirt. After all, he's only a man, she thought fiercely. What can he know about a girl's dreams!

'God,' he muttered. 'I don't understand what you do to

me, Peabody. We'd better go into the house and—tears? Why?'

She sniffed back the last drop, and used a knuckle to clear her eyes.

'Why?' he repeated.

'Nothing,' she stuttered. 'Sometimes women feel like crying. It isn't every day that—that one gets a proposal—or—oh lord, I can't hold it in!' The tears came again. She wrestled free from his embrace and raced back to the house as fast as her feet could carry her. Blinded, she fumbled her way down the hall and into the kitchen, where George was still at work.

'Why, what's the matter?' the old man asked, as he opened his arms and Phil came into them.

'I—Penn and I——' she stammered through the tears. 'We're going to be married.'

'Which is certainly a good reason for a girl to cry her heart out,' Mr Yu murmured, laughing over Phil's bent head.

Penn made all the arrangements. Or perhaps his super-efficient secretary did. In any event on Monday Doctor Hanson came to the house, took a blood sample, gave her a smile of approval, and went off mumbling to himself about laboratory schedules and tons of work to be done. But Harry, who drove the doctor to the house, gave Phil a wink as if assuring her that all medical men have such troubles.

And so when Rose came to her at one o'clock in the afternoon with a puzzled frown on her face, Phil saw no real problem. 'So if your niece is that sick,' she assured the cook, 'Frank can drive you down to San Francisco right away. No, it's no real problem. Harry said he and—

Penn—would be home early, and Mr Yu is out at the back somewhere.'

Frank managed to combine his errands. He took Cecily home on the way, and promised to stay in the city until Rose was sure he was not needed.

That left Phil rumbling around the house until Robbie came in from school at two o'clock, with Mary, the afternoon maid, right behind him. At which time, Philomena told herself, somebody has to get dinner for the master of the house, and that somebody is obviously me. And off she went to the kitchen.

She heard the noise in the front hall at about three o'clock. The big front door slammed, and feet echoed down the hall. A quick smile flashed across Phil's face. She wiped flour off her hands on to one of Rose's super-sized aprons. Penn was home earlier than she had expected. Her hands fumbled with the ties of the apron. Ordinarily when she was cooking she thought nothing of welcoming guests in an apron. But Penn, on the day before their wedding? Nothing doing! She struggled, but the loop around her neck got caught in her hair, and it was a pretty dishevelled housekeeper who finally made it to the hall. It wasn't Penn.

Mary stood in the alcove leading into the library, a strange couple stood at the foot of the stairs, and Robbie was frozen in position half way down.

The woman was tall and aristocratic, her blonde hair piled up on her head in the latest fashion, wearing a mink coat despite the heat. The man was tall, thin, trying to hide a narrow face behind a full beard and moustache. Not one of that kind, Phil moaned, as she positioned herself between Robbie and the intruders.

'And you are?' she inquired in her best deep voice.

'Oh, none of your business,' the woman stated flatly. 'I don't have to dispute the world with the hired help. Come, Robbie, we're leaving at once.'

'No,' the boy shouted, backing up the stairs. 'They can't make me go, Phil?'

'No, they can't make you go,' she answered.

'I'm the boy's mother,' the woman snapped. 'Come down here, Robert. At once, do you hear.'

'So that's it,' Philomena grated. 'Possession is nine points of the law? Well, Mrs whatever your name is now, *that's* the boy's mother.' She gestured over her shoulder to the picture that gleamed against the wall. 'And there's no way you're going to get Robbie out of this house without his father's approval.'

'We don't have to put up with this nonsense,' the woman returned. 'Donald. Get the boy. Now.'

'Mary, call the police. Report an attempted kidnapping,' Phil called. All eyes turned to the maid. She was standing just by the hall telephone, but made no effort to pick it up.

'Eloise?'

It was obvious that Donald really didn't want to play the game. 'Get the boy,' the woman snapped. 'They're all alone in the house.' She turned her attention back to Phil. 'And don't think we don't know about you. Living in his house. In the next room, for that matter. You just wait until the Judge hears about *this*. We've got pictures!'

Donald had finally made up his mind. He moved past Eloise and headed for the stairs. Phil backed up directly in front of him, slowing him down. 'Robbie,' she called over her shoulder. 'Into your room. Lean out the window and yell for Mr Yu.'

Donald stopped, one foot in the air. 'Mr Yu?' he asked over his shoulder.

'The Chinese gardener,' Eloise supplied. 'He's eighty years old at least.'

Robbie had gone by this time, his boots clattering on the stairs as if heralding the Light Brigade. Donald put his foot down on the next riser. Phil backed up slowly, directly in front of him. 'You'd better change your mind, Donald,' she told him softly. 'You're the one who's going to get hurt. Although when I get through with you I might save up a punch or two for your lovely wife. That would sound good in court, wouldn't it?'

He hesitated again. 'Get on with it,' his wife ordered. He began the pursuit. This is silly, Phil told herself. Here I am being stalked by a rabbit! But he is big. What I need is a weapon. They were in the second-floor corridor, inching gradually down toward Robbie's room. She could hear the boy yelling out of the window at the top of his lungs. His bedroom door was open. Phil backed into the room, and found exactly what she needed.

It was something one finds in every American child's bedroom, girl or boy, when they get to a certain age. A baseball bat. She hefted it, found the balance, and moved briskly back to the door. 'Don't bother, Robbie,' she called over her shoulder. 'Everything's in good order now.'

'That's what you think.' The man in the door was trying to show a little bravado. He hadn't seen the bat as yet. 'I intend to take that brat with me, little girl, and— oooh.' The bat, wielded like a quarter-staff, had just slammed into his solar plexus. He dropped to the floor, gasping for breath.

More footsteps clattered on the stairs. High heels.

Eloise stormed down the corridor, her face rigid with anger. 'Get up, Donald, and get that child,' she screamed. 'Donald? What happened to——?'

'You'd better pick him up and go home,' Phil grinned at her. 'Donald has suddenly decided not to do any kidnapping today.' The worn end of the bat wiggled in her hands. Eloise carefully started to back down the hall.

'You'd better take Donald with you,' Phil insisted. 'They don't collect garbage in our neighbourhood for another two days.'

'I—wait until I tell the judge about this,' Eloise threatened. 'Now I'm sure we'll get custody of the boy.' She had been sliding steadily towards the stairs, ready to abandon her new husband, when she backed into George Yu.

The old man had sufficient strength to force Eloise back up the hall, and sufficient wit to take in all the evidence. 'Kidnappers,' he chuckled. 'You want me to use judo on them? I could break a few bones?'

Eloise paled, her face so white that the patches of rouge on her cheeks gleamed like fire. 'No, no,' she gasped. 'We're going. It was all a terrible mistake. Get up, Donald.'

Donald looked as if he would rather stay where he was, but when Mr Yu bent over towards him he scuttled along the floor a few paces and staggered to his feet. The Chinese gardener pointed toward the door, and the pair of them fled. The three conspirators waited until they heard the front door slam, and then broke into laughter.

'Would you really use judo?' Phil asked through the giggles.

'Me?' the old man returned. 'What do I know about judo? I spent all my life in California. Baseball I know—

judo, no. That's Japanese stuff. Besides, what did you need me for? I was busy with the camellia beds. Exhibition next month. I *have* to get the blossoms ready.'

'Well, I'm sorry,' Phil said very primly. 'I couldn't find the baseball bat, you see.'

Mr Yu smiled, bowed, and retreated down the hall. He moved like a shadow, without a noise. What a marvellous man, Phil told herself, and then, unable to contain it, told Robbie, 'He'd make a wonderful grandfather.'

'Mr Yu?'

'Who else?'

'Why did you do that?' the boy asked. 'You didn't have to fight him just for me. He was a lot bigger than you.'

'Yeah,' she giggled, 'but I had the bat.'

'And you did it just for me?'

'Just for you. Hurts, does it?'

'Yeah. Sort of. I'm not accustomed to——' That tiny smile edged at the corners of his mouth. He saw his reflection in the wall-mirror and quickly replaced the smile with his normal frown.

Philomena whistled as she took the stairs two at a time, stopping to pay tribute to the Pirate King, and Robbie's mother. Mary was struggling into her coat by the front door.

'Leaving?'

'I—I guess I'd better,' the maid replied. 'I——'

'I know. You've been spying on us for them all the time.' There was no bitterness in Phil's voice. She understood the woman's need. 'They paid you to call them?'

'Yes. I—I needed the money. I hate to lose my job. It's the baby.'

'Yes. I know all about it, Mary. I looked into it all last Friday. It wasn't such a terrible crime, what you did, provided it doesn't happen again. There's no need to give up your job—unless you can't stand us here.'

'No need to——?'

'No need to. And next week, when things settle down, I want you to sit down with Mr Wilderman and see if he can't work something out. I know it's all been a shock. Go on home. Take a few days off, and come back when you're ready. Nobody need know except you and I, and I have the most atrocious memory you ever saw.'

There were genuine tears in the woman's eyes. She thought for a moment, nodded her head, and turned to the door. 'I'll be back Wednesday,' she said softly, and went out.

'And that leaves the whole blinking house to me,' Phil lectured herself. There was a smell invading the hall. 'Oh my heavens,' she wailed as she ran for the kitchen. 'My pies!'

There was no need for her elaborately prepared explanation, concocted over a tray of hot biscuits to go with the salmon loaf. Robbie clattered down the stairs as soon as Penn's car purred to a halt, and poured the whole story into his ear before Phil could even get her apron off.

Dinner went well, but there were so many questions to be answered that Phil hardly managed a bite before everyone else was finished. The whole affair was topped off when Frank stomped into the house in the middle of the meal.

'Wasn't any emergency at all,' he grunted. 'Nothing wrong with anybody in Rose's family. Somebody's playing games with the telephone. Rose nearly blew a fuse when she found out. I brought her back and left her at home.'

Later that night, exhausted, Phil tumbled out of the shower, slipped into her shorty nightgown, and stood by the window to watch the full moon chase the evening star across the sky. Up in the mountains, forty miles away, it was snowing. Down in the protected valley where the Sacramento and the American rivers flowed, spring was showing signs. By craning her head she could see the reflected light of the dome of the State Capitol. And this is how the rich people live, she chuckled to herself. Here I am in the middle of the city and it looks more like country living than actually being out in the country.

Behind her there was a light knock on the interconnecting door. She left the view behind her reluctantly. There was no need for a robe—Penn couldn't see anything. She opened the door and extended her hand.

'What are you doing?' he asked casually.

'Just looking—the window,' she murmured. He came to her as if he had all his faculties, slipping one arm around her waist, and walking her back to the window. There was nothing at all wrong with his sense of touch, she told herself, alarmed. His hand was broadly open, resting in that declivity where her narrow waist swelled outwards into her rounded hip. His finger tips moved.

Not a sweeping caress, just a sensuous application and release of pressure, almost as if he were playing a drum. And if his fingers were the drummer, her skin came taut under the pressure, as if she were the drum.

'So you hit Donald with the baseball bat,' he murmured into her mass of hair.

'Well, it seemed the logical thing to do at the time,' she

returned. 'She said—that it would help *their* case in court.
I hope it doesn't?'

'I don't think it will,' he reassured her. 'The more I
think of it the funnier it all seems.'

The conversation seemed to be going on at two levels.
The verbal she could handle—if she put her mind to it.
The other, the pleasing assault of his fingertips, was
beyond her experience, and her automatic response,
moving closer against his side, did nothing to help her
resolution. Her nightgown, lightweight, felt almost as if
it were not there. His hand rested just inches above its
hem. She felt a crazily mixed feeling—remorse and
relief—when it lifted and moved higher. And gasped as it
kept going upwards, to rest on the lower slope of her
breast. And the conversation went on.

'Tomorrow is our wedding-day.' A casual statement of
fact from him that caused her mind to somersault. In all
the madness of the day she had forgotten!

'Yes——' she managed to stammer, 'Yes, it is. I—I
hope the weather's nice.'

'That's my girl,' he laughed. 'Tomorrow is our
wedding-day and you want to talk about the weather?'

'It—it seemed to be the safest subject.'

'Ah. I never thought of you as wanting to be safe.'

'Well, I do,' she insisted. 'Every woman does. It isn't
the same for a woman as for a man.'

'What isn't?'

'Getting married. It's too wrapped up in responsibili-
ties and—and passions——'

'I understand.' Those pernicious fingers smoothed the
firmness of her breast, touched lightly on its proud peak,
and faded away. Regretfully.

'I just wanted to say good night. Everything will be all

right, Philomena. I shall keep you safe. Guide me back to
the door.'

'I know you will,' she sighed as she led him back to his
own room. There was no sleep to be had that night. She
tossed and turned, feeling the trail of those fingers all
night long, wishing mightily that there could have been
no need for him to stop.

She came down to breakfast with him on Tuesday,
before he went off to work. They were all quiet. Robbie
squirmed in his chair, almost smiling. Harry was his
usually gloomy self, and Penn seemed to be wrapped up
in something deep in his mind. As she had done for
weeks now, Phil picked up the morning paper and began
to read him the headlines. But none of the stories caught
his interest, and when she stopped short of the whole
reading, he didn't urge her on.

'I'll send the car for you,' he told her briefly. 'Along
about midday, I suppose, and I'll meet you there.'

She stood in the door for ten minutes after the car had
gone. What a wedding, she groaned to herself. I'll meet
you there. Well, I suppose when you stretch the truth a
little, that's what happens at a *normal* wedding, right?
The groom waits at the church, and the bride comes to
him. *Normal*, hah!

So it was all rather a surprise when the doorbell went at
about ten-thirty, and Cecily, a big smile on her face,
ushered her sister Sally into the living-room. Sister Sally
and half a million packages.

'Well, you certainly fooled us all,' her sister said as she
slumped down on the couch to catch her breath. 'Lord,
I've been running around like a head with its chicken cut
off. That man is crazy, Phil.'

'That man?'

'That man that you're going to marry. Now we'd better try everything on. Mrs Ralston is waiting just in case something needs to be adjusted.'

'Mrs Ralston? Waiting where?'

'She's the head seamstress from Balmain's, silly——'

'And she's up in your bedroom,' Cecily interrupted. 'And she don't look like a wait-around person.'

'But you——' Phil sighed as she took her youngest sister's hands. 'Stop just right there. What the devil is this all about?'

'Well, you could have knocked me over with a feather when he telephoned me yesterday morning. Of course I had all your measurements. So he sent that sexy car around after me, and he and I went down to Balmain's—boy, is he a choosy guy. It took hours. For me they never would have stirred a stump. For him they jumped every time he opened his mouth. What the devil does he do—own a gold-mine?'

'Several dozen,' practical Phil inserted deftly. 'And I still don't know what you're talking about. Let's go upstairs—at least we shan't keep Mrs Ralston waiting for whatever it is.'

Her bedroom had been taken over. Mrs Ralston had brought two assistants, who were busy emptying boxes, and stuffing their contents into her wardrobe, and her bureaux. Noting her anxious look, the seamstress said, 'Your future husband insisted on a complete trousseau, Miss Peabody. A little of everything, he specified. And this, of course.'

A dressmaker's dummy stood by the open window, and Phil's heart did a sudden jump at the dress it displayed. Orange blossom and white lace, demurely seductive, revealing a little, promising everything. She could almost hear the wedding march being played in the background. A tiny gold coronet—pure gold it would be—the idea broke through her trance, and left her giggling like a fool. A long train, the veil, everything! It was too hard not to cry—and when she started they all joined in—all except Mrs Ralston, who had other things on her mind.

A few alterations were required. Well, Mrs Ralston thought they were, and Phil had given up the struggle long since. It was easier to just drift down with the tide. 'Just a little lower in the cleavage,' the dressmaker insisted.

'A little more and I'll get pneumonia,' Phil protested feebly.

'The lace will protect you,' the practical answer came. Sure, Phil thought. The lace was like a transparent film, hardly real enough to stand a fingerprint. Sure it will protect me. You bet!

And when it was finally completed, they all insisted she take it off again. And come down to lunch!

'I couldn't eat a thing,' she sighed for the tenth time.

'Got the willies?' Sally laughed. 'Me too. But if you think it's bad now, wait until tonight!' They all laughed.

'Very funny,' Phil groaned.

'So eat something,' Rose insisted. 'It takes a lot of strength to be a bride.'

'Yeah, sure.' But she did manage a pink grapefruit, the smallest corner of the steak she was served, and a piece of toast. 'And Penn did all this?' she asked again.

'All this,' her sister assured her. 'With his fingers, no less. He felt everything from top to bottom, then had me describe the whole ensemble. What a lucky girl you are, Sis. You just wait until he gets those pads off his eyes.

Now, I've got to change too. Upstairs, lady.'

'You too? For a wedding in a——' Shut up, Phil, she yelled at herself. You don't know what's going on. Just shut up and do what you're told. You just wait until he gets those pads off his eyes—yeah. You're not what he thinks you are, and nobody, but nobody fools around with Penn Wilderman's sensibilities! There'll be a day of reckoning, little Miss Peabody! She shivered, and Mrs Ralston complained of it as they slipped the magic dress down over her head again, set the train, adjusted the veil, flounced out the fulness of it all, and led her gently down the stairs. The limousine was waiting.

'There'll be a reckoning,' she told herself as she stepped carefully into the big interior. 'But not today, lady. Enjoy.'

The car whispered away, like a magic carpet. She closed her eyes. For some reason she didn't want to see where the judge's chambers were. The ride was longer than she had expected, and the bridal party was tense. The bridal party. Herself, Sally, Cecily, and Rose. Mrs Ralston had gathered all her troops and disappeared.

'We're here.' Sally made the announcement, nudging her sister. Phil opened her eyes. 'It isn't the guillotine,' Sally chuckled. 'Or if it is, you're riding in one fancy tumbril, sis. Get moving. We're five minutes late. And I don't think the man you're marrying is much of a waiter-around either.'

And so she opened her eyes. The car was parked directly in front of her own parish church, Saint Clement's Episcopal. The doors were wide open, waiting. Sally handed her the tiny bouquet of orange blossom, they all fussed with her dress and veil, the organ sounded, and she walked down the aisle towards the

altar, where he and Harry and Robbie waited, all kitted
out in formal wear. Her arm shook in the crook of Mr
Yu's elbow. Her entire frame shivered until that moment
when she came close enough to feel the aura, and Mr Yu
transferred her hand into that of Penn. Then suddenly it
all became a dream, a warm comforting dream, and the
shivers left her.

The ceremony passed completely over her head. She
must have made the proper answers, because the organ
was playing again, and Penn was folding back her veil to
kiss her. She walked back down the aisle with him, proud
and puzzled. At the door of the church he stopped and
kissed her again.

'What's the trouble, Philomena?' he asked softly.

'I—I was surprised,' she sighed. 'The dress, the
church. I thought we—you—I was just surprised.'

'I'm not altogether insensitive,' he whispered in her
ear. Her hands crept up around his neck, and she pulled
his head down to hers.

'Thank you for everything.' And the tears came in little
driblets.

'Crying on your wedding-day?' he teased. 'I thought
only the bride's mother did that. What's the matter now?

'I—nothing,' she mumbled, and ducked her head into
his shirt front. She had finally puzzled it all out. What a
stupid place this was to discover that you've fallen in love
with your husband!

CHAPTER EIGHT

THE party was a small one. The group of Penn's friends who had been at the church came home with them. Sally's husband Jim had joined, apologising for missing the ceremony. The old house welcomed her. It seemed to smile, gap-toothed, through its arches at her. Confused, wildly happy and at home, she needed a clean up and a respite from the tight coronet that held her veil. When she went up the lady in the picture smiled at her.

'Wish me luck,' Phil begged as Sally hustled her up the stairs.

'Who, me? I already did that.'

'Not you, sis. The girl in the picture. I have a sort of feeling that if——'

'Don't let it worry you, love. Look at that leer on the Pirate's face, over here. Now if *he* got you alone in some dark corner you'd have something to worry about!'

Phil dappled her face with cold water while her sister looked over the room in awe. With coronet and veil off, she took down her hair, brushing it out into a gleaming sheath of wild curls. 'Be careful of the dress,' Cecily admonished, giggling. 'You'll need it for your daughter.'

'Yes. Of course.' Why not dream? Phil challenged herself. What law is it that says I can't delude myself if I want to? And so she stood carefully still while her two attendants rearranged the beautiful wedding-gown. One question bothered her, and she could not help but ask. 'How did you know about the wedding, Sally?'

'The wedding? Your—Penn, is it?—Penn telephoned.'
And then, in a more serious tone, 'Deborah had already
gone. They found a baby-sitter for the week, and took off
for Lake Tahoe.'

'Who in the world would willingly watch those two for
a week?'

'John's mother and father. I don't say they were happy
to do it, but they're doing it.'

'And Samantha?'

'I—I'm sorry, Phil. Samantha and her husband have
decided that you are purposely keeping them from *her*
inheritance. Sam said—well, she wouldn't come. And
after all you did for them! Dammit, Phil, sometimes
relatives can be worse than enemies!'

'Don't let it bother you,' Phil said softly. 'I'll survive,
and one day they'll get over it. You'll see. Hadn't we
better go down?'

The group downstairs was making enough noise for
twice its number. Phil hesitated on the bottom stair, took
a couple of deep breaths to steady her nerves, and strode
into the living-room looking as complacent as if she had
done this sort of thing every day. Or at least once a week,
she amended as they all turned in her direction and her
composure slipped away from her.

Penn was standing in the middle of the room, a glass in
his hand, his ears perked. 'Philomena?' She went directly
to him, a rush of affection assaulting her. He smiled
when she stretched high enough to kiss the tip of his nose,
then surrounded her with one arm. Somebody in the
crowd filled her hand with a chilled champagne glass.

'A toast,' Penn announced. 'To the loveliest bride ever
to come into the Wilderman family.' There were cheers
as the wine went down. Not used to wine at all, Phil

emptied her glass, and then hiccupped as the sparkling liquid hit her stomach. Penn pulled her close. 'What did you say?' he whispered in her ear.

She hiccupped once more. 'What I said,' she whispered back, 'is that you haven't the slightest idea what you're talking about, Mr Wilderman.' Someone filled her glass. She clinked it against his. 'And here's a toast to the true descendant of the Pirate King,' she whispered back at him. The second glass went down as quickly as her first, but nobody was counting—or noticing—until he handed his glass into the nearest passing hands and swooped down on her with both arms. Her own glass fell to the floor, and there was considerable cheering as his lips touched hers gently, moved away, and then almost as if compelled by outside forces, came back passionately, demandingly, sweeping her out of herself with sweet abandon. It left her weak, trembling, leaning against him for support. He gathered her up again, coddling her head against his chest gently.

'And that's what happens to uppity wives,' he whispered into her hair. 'Want to try for two?'

'I wouldn't dare,' she quavered. 'Not here, with all these people watching!'

'Now that's the right attitude,' he chuckled, releasing her. She didn't want to go. 'We have to mingle,' he chided.

'I—I'd rather do it right where I am,' she confessed, but he gently pushed her away, and she mingled.

An hour later they had all gone. Rose provided a buffet supper for the family. The lobster was delightful, the heart-of-palm salad equal to it, but everything else Phil noted was some hazy world whose borders were too ill-defined for her to recognise them. Never-never Land, she asked herself? What have I done to me? She was seated between Penn and Robbie, and they both looked so—so huge, so handsome, so——

'So now *you're* my mother.' Robbie, bending close to her ear.

'It looks as if,' she returned, having trouble with all the syllables. 'Eat your heart out, kid.' The lobster salad splattered all over her beautiful dress.

'I dunno,' the boy chuckled. 'I like neat people.'

'What are you two arguing about?'

'We're not arguing, Penn. We never argue. We occasionaly—did I say that right?—we fight might, but we don't argue.'

'How much champagne have you had tonight, Philomena?'

'Counting this one?'

'Yes, counting that one.'

She gulped it down thirstily and giggled as the bubbles tickled her nose. 'That makes—three,' she managed. They were both laughing, and she could see nothing funny about it at all, as her earnest face showed. 'Compared to all the champagne you've drunk in your lifetime, that's hardly a drop, love.' She shivered at the word. Love. Delicious. If only it were true. Why is my mind so hazy?

She wanted to be sure he understood her. 'Yes, three,' she said sleepily.

'Yes,' Penn chuckled. 'I understand. You're sleepy, and you've had three glasses of champagne tonight.'

'No, no.' She waved her hand in front of his face to get his attention. 'I've had three all of my life. Only two tonight.'

She had spent the whole evening sitting up straight,

being the lady. And now suddenly the table was at an angle, falling slowly up at her. Things were all just very confusing. The salad bowl kept falling up at her, faster and faster, until Robbie yelled, and Penn caught her by the shoulders, then climbed out of his chair and swung her up in his arms. 'Whoever would have thought of it. She doesn't drink alcohol. Wow!' He shifted her weight in his arms, so that her head rested on his shoulder. One of her arms was around his neck, and a contented smile marked her face.

'She's smiling,' Robbie said softly.

'Is she really? Well, we've got to get her to bed, Robbie. It'll have to be a two-man job. I'll carry and you guide. Right?'

'Right.' They started slowly for the stairs, doing each tread slowly. Half-way up one of those huge eyes of hers opened.

'Penn,' she managed, waving towards the painting. 'Who was that lady?'

He stopped, shifting her weight again, looking over his shoulder. 'I thought I told you before,' he said gently. 'That's my sister Robin.'

That's my sister. That *was* my sister. *That's my mother,* Robbie had said. The words haunted her confused mind. She squeezed the eye shut again and tried to move closer to him.

'Stop wriggling,' he complained softly. 'You'll have us both back down the stairs. I'm not one of these macho Hollywood stunt men.' She became rigid in his arms, which made it worse, and then went limp as he carried her into her room and stretched her out gently on the bed. They *shushed* each other as the door closed behind them.

She squeezed one eye open. 'Shower,' she muttered.

'Wedding night.' The floor rocked abominably, but she made it to the bathroom, shedding items of clothing as she went.

With more luck than skill she managed to cram her curls under her shower cap, and stepped into the cubicle. The hot water sprayed ice-cold, shocking her out of her comfortable daze. Her blank mind began to spin, and even the gradual warming of the water could not help.

'Wedding-night,' she muttered. 'Happily ever after!' The thought twisted like a knife to her heart. He had already set the boundaries to their marriage. Just until he could see again. It would have worked, she thought bitterly, if I hadn't gone and fallen in love with him. Now *that's* a real laugher, Philomena. Poor slow-witted Philomena.

One day soon he'll be able to see again. What will he expect? An old battle-axe? Five-foot-two of stern matriarch? You little fool. He doesn't even know how tall you are. Five foot two, provided you wear two-inch heels. Grey hair. How can he possibly know that it's straw-blonde, that the curls are real, not ironed in? He's braille-read my face, but all he knows is that it's round. He can't tell that I've got green eyes, and a dimple in each cheek. And a too-wide mouth that couldn't be stern if it wanted to. What a mess!

She shut off the water and stepped out into the steamy bathroom. The full-length mirror on the wall confronted her with more than she wanted to see. No, he can't know all that, her mind screamed at her. That's something he'll never see. The freckles on my shoulders, and across the bridge of my nose. The pale white skin that burns when I'm not careful. The full, firm breasts. If I were older he would expect *something* to sag a little?

The narrow waist? No, I stopped him when he got that far in his *research*. The comfortable hips, the tapered legs? Nothing. He'll look for a woman of comfortable age, inches taller than I am, and he'll pass over the little thing I really am, with all my fears and prejudices and *ordinariness* written on my face, and he—and he won't even know me. Or want to know me. And that's what will break your heart, won't it, Philomena Wilderman? Her mind was too muzzy, too filled with fears and tears to continue. She dabbed at herself with the towel, discarded the shower cap, and stumbled back to bed.

The pale light of pre-dawn was outlining the window when she woke up. She was lying flat on her back in her own bed. See, she told herself, you went and got yourself fool-drunk, and nothing bad happened. Here you are, totally naked in your own bed—totally naked? The thought startled her, and she tried to sit up. It proved impossible. A heavy brown arm was thrown completely across her body, locking her into position. The attached hand had taken complete possession of her left breast. When she tried to gently remove it there was an instant groan of protest in her ear. She inched her head sidewise, and found herself nose to nose with a man.

It was something she had not expected. Something she had not even thought about. Which proves what an idiot you are, Philomena Peabody, she lectured herself. She wriggled slightly to try to break away. The movement brought another protest, and the hand slowly and gently kneaded her breast, until its roseate peak sprang to full proud life. It brought something else too, a wild incessant hammering at the door behind which she had locked all her passions. And just another minute of this, she knew, would show how weak that lock was. She froze in position again. The hand gradually came to a stop. She stared at the pads that covered his eyes, wishing mightily she might see them without them seeing her.

What have I done? Nothing unusual, her practical mind insisted. That's not just a man—that's your husband. You remember, Phil? Orange blossoms and lace, and *I, Philomena take thee, Penn.* Remember? Harry couldn't find the ring because Robbie had it, and Cecily caught the bouquet, and you stepped out into the sunlight, right in the church doors, and discovered you loved him? Remember? Well, there he is. The man in possession. He's the *possessor,* and you're the *possessee,* lady, and there's no way to back out of it—because you don't want to! He needs a shave. He's got such a heavy beard. Funny I had't noticed that before. I wonder how it feels to kiss a man with a beard? Well, it's not really a beard, just a little—lord, isn't it rough! That was her two fingers, exploring, reporting, drawing back quickly when the dragon almost opened an eye. And we're in my bed together, and it's almost morning and he—good lord, he's as naked as I am!

So what I'll do, she decided, is to lie here quietly, making believe I'm fast asleep, until he—but he didn't. Not for another three hours, and by that time Phil was indeed sound asleep again, dreaming wild dreams, sighing sweetly in the toils of the dragon.

On Wednesday morning it was another noise, another male, who brought her up out of the darkness. Sleepily she forced one eye open. Robbie was sitting on the foot of the bed, bouncing. The mattress shook.

'Hey,' the boy called. 'Dad's downtown. He called and told me to get you up. They've moved the hearing up a day. We have to be in court by eleven o'clock!' She gave him a glare and then a smile, and pushed him in the general direction of her door.

She dressed slowly. What does one wear to a court hearing in the morning? Something judgmental? Dark, sober? Her hand reached automatically for one of her two old light blue trouser-suits. Her office uniform, no less. But a sudden intuition stopped her. Instead she chose a demure white blouse with a Peter Pan collar, and imitation gold studs at the wrists. A sturdy corduroy beige skirt, and a pair of dark brown half-boots completed the outfit. She brushed her mass of hair diligently, and let it hang free. A touch of pink lipgloss, a bit of powder on her nose, and she was ready. 'Into the valley of death——' she quoted haphazardly as she squared her shoulders and went down.

The hearing was to be held in rooms in the Hall of Justice, 'because of alterations in the regular Juvenile court,' Frank explained. They drove down I street, past the City Hall and the Post Office. There was construction everywhere. The city was growing almost before her eyes. Which she could open now, she found. The aspirin had already begun its work. There wasn't a parking place to be had. So what else is new, she asked herself.

Frank drove the limousine right up to the front of the building, parked in the No Parking zone, and held the door for them. Harry was waiting for them on the steps. 'The boss has gone up already,' he said. 'He and the lawyer. Better hurry up. This judge, she don't stand for nonsense.' He took the crook of Phil's arm and hustled her up and into the building.

'She?'

'Yeah. Judge Irene Mulrooney. Not too well liked by

the lawyers. She doesn't care for long-running cases.'

'Like this one.'

'Yeah. Like this one. You don't look old enough to be married, Mrs Wilderman.'

'Well!' It was all she could think to say. Twice in one hour. Well! She squared her shoulders and reached back for Robbie's hand. It came into hers. Reluctantly, but it came.

The hearing room was larger than she had expected, but plain. A bare desk in the middle of the room for the judge, with a high-backed swivel chair, and two sets of modern armchairs, facing each other on opposite sides. The empty space in the middle looked like the bullring, waiting. Blood spilled? she asked herself. Will it be one of *those* battles?

Penn knew she was there. Perhaps the sound of her heels, she considered. But she was wearing boots, and the heels were soft leather. But he knew, and he stood up, a smile on his face, and arms extended.

For the audience, she supposed. The opposite side of the room was crowded. Eloise and Donald, and what must have been a whole platoon of lawyers, all glaring at her. Play the game, she told herself fiercely. Play the game.

Her feet did not require orders. They sped up, leaving Harry behind, and in a moment she was safe again, squeezed inside his arms, almost as if it were all true. It *is* all true, she insisted to herself. It is! We're married—and even if only one of us is in love, there's enough here for two. More than enough. Her sigh gave her away.

'Something bothering?' His lips were at her ear.

'I—I don't know,' she sighed. 'I think I—I'm just not a morning person—and changing the date surprised me. I don't like surprises. I like—neat, orderly—well, sometimes I do.'

'Sounds a little confusing there,' he chuckled. 'I'll see what I can do about providing a safe orderly life for you.'

'Can you do that?' she sighed.

'You sound suspicious.'

'I don't know a great deal about *happily ever after*,' she confessed, pressing her nose into his chest. There might have been more lovely words, but at that moment Robbie caught up to them, exchanged a very adult handshake with his father, and sat down. Harry pre-empted the lawyer's seat in the first row, and relegated that worthy to the second row. Penn offered a brief introduction. 'Mr Whirlmount,' he nodded backward. Phil barely caught a look at the middle-aged blue-eyed man behind them, before Penn seized on her attention, drawing her down beside him.

She scanned his face for some sign that he knew yesterday had been different, and last night had—what? Those gauze pads stared back at her.

'Are you peeking?'

'With these things on? Don't be silly.'

'Did you get your eyedrops this morning?'

'Is this what it means to be married?'

'Yes, it does,' she snapped indignantly. 'I'm entitled to worry about you!'

'Yes. I admit that,' he laughed. 'One of the pads fell off last night. Harry fixed everything this morning.'

'One of them fell off?' Panic. Last night? She squirmed in her chair. 'What—what did you see?'

'A dark night,' he whispered. 'Was there something I should have seen?'

'Oh no!' The judge and bailiff came in at that moment.

She jumped to her feet, spilling her purse and its contents
all over the floor. The judge looked over at her as she bent
to recapture her wordly goods. Judge Mulrooney. About
sixty, white-haired, gold-rimmed glasses, tall for a
woman. She nodded at both sides of the case with equal
chill, and sat down. Phil, still scrambling for her lipstick
and key-chain, half under the chairs, decided to leave
things where they were. She stood up, brushed down her
skirts, blushed an apology at the judge, and sank into the
chair next to Penn, hoping she might sink competely out
of sight. The judge rapped on the desk top with the
rounded end of a ballpoint pen. Her recorder rushed in
and handed her a large envelope. She opened it with
some disdain. 'The Case of Wilderman Versus Wilderman,' the judge announced. Her court recorder bent over
her shoulder and whispered in her ear.

'I stand corrected. The case is amended to read
Wilderman versus Worth. Do I understand, madam, that
you are the former Mrs Wilderman and are now Mrs
Donald Worth?' Eloise's platoon of lawyers signalled
agreement.

'I'm sure she can speak for herself,' the judge
commented wryly.

'Yes,' Eloise returned. Her voice was high and shrill,
on the point of breaking.

'And your former husband, Mr Wilderman, is suing
for custody of an adopted child, Robert Penn
Wilderman.'

'Yes,' Penn nodded.

'You, Mr Wilderman, charge your former wife with
neglect, child-abuse, and failure to comply with prior
court orders. Now, let me hear the lawyers.' And she did.
For an hour and thirty minutes, like a battle royal, as Phil

slipped lower and lower in her chair, trying to dodge the verbal bullets. The judge handled them skilfully. Probed, when questions seemed half answered. Tapped her pen occasionally when things seemed to be getting out of order. And then——

'And now, Mrs Worth, I see you have added to your charges, alleging that your former husband is now, along with his other problems, guilty of lewd and lascivious conduct, by reason of living openly and immorally with another woman. Who?'

'That one. Right there,' Eloise screamed. 'They've been at it for weeks, with the boy in the house too!'

'Well,' the judge sighed. 'What is the quotation—there are none so blind as those who will not see? You, young lady. Are you cohabiting with the plaintiff?'

'Me?' Phil squeaked. 'Am I what?'

'Are you living in the same house as Mr Wilderman there?'

'I—yes.'

'All right, sit down, I won't bite you.'

The devil you won't, Phil sighed. Penn's hand closed on hers again, gently. It did a little bit to soothe her spirit, but not much. The judge was tapping her pen on the desk monotonously.

'I think I understand everything so far,' Judge Mulrooney said softly. 'So now we'll hear from the third party involved. Robert Wilderman?'

The lawyer reached over the row of chairs and tapped Robbie on the shoulder. The boy stood up. In spite of the suit, the tie, he looked like an accident on its way to happen. That sullen teenage scowl was back in full force. He spared one quick look over his shoulder at Phil, and she could see the unspoken appeal in his eyes. She shifted over to be as close to him as possible. He heard the chair shift, and one of his hands reached behind his back. Phil leaned forward and tucked her own in his. It continued to surprise her. Thirteen years old, and his hand was bigger than hers. Bigger and stronger. It closed around her like a vice. The boy backed up, as close to his chair as he could get, and hung on.

'Robert Penn Wilderman?'

'Yes sir—ma'am.'

'Don't be embarrassed. What do your friends call you?'

'Robbie.'

'Well then, Robbie. You've lived with your mother, the present Mrs Worth.'

'She's not my mother. My mother is——' The bitterness rolled out of him. The judge tapped the desk.

'Yes, I understand that. But Mrs Worth is your mother by adoption, as your uncle has now become your father by adoption.'

'That's it!' Phil clamped her hand over her mouth as everyone in the court glared at her. But that was it. She remembered. He was carrying her up the stairs, when they looked at the painting. *That's my mother, Robbie had said*. And *that's my sister, Penn had said*. No wonder they look alike. He's not—how could I have thought that Robbie was his illegitimate child! How could I have thought that! She wanted so badly to apologise to the silent man sitting straight and true beside her, but the judge was watching.

'To continue,' Judge Mulrooney said, 'If I may, young lady?'

'Yes. I—I'm sorry,' Phil stammered.

'And then, Robbie, you lived with your father for some time?'

A very defensive, 'Yes.'

'Now, Robbie, there are three sides to this case. It's your life we are dealing with. You *do* understand that?'

'Yes, ma'am.'

'Good. Now, given your own choice, Robbie, would you prefer to live with your mother?'

'Her? No. I don't want to live with her. She hates me. Her and that—that wimp she married.' More taps with the pen.

'All she's interested in is that I need to be living in her house at the end of each quarter, because that's when the company pays my dividends, and she takes all the money. That's all she's interested in, my money. I'd let her have it all if I didn't have to live with her.'

'All right, son. Mrs Worth, is it true that you receive all the child's stock dividends? One eighth of the company stock?' The judge peered at some papers. 'Eighty thousand dollars a year?'

'Well, I—yes,' Eloise began. 'But you know how expensive it is to feed a child these days.'

'Yes, I'm sure I do,' the judge snapped. 'I have three myself. Eighty thousand dollars. How much of that is banked for the boy's future?'

'Banked?' Eloise's troops were in confusion, muttering among themselves.

'Well?'

'None, your honour,' her lawyer interjected.

'But next year we expect to start an investment programme for him,' Eloise shrilled. 'My—Mr Worth is an Investment Counsellor.'

'Next year?' The judge grinned. There was nothing

happy about it. It looked like the grin a wolf might offer when meeting Little Red Riding Hood.

'All right, Robbie,' she continued. 'So you would prefer to live with your father?'

The boy agonised for a moment, then shook his head negatively. 'No,' he managed. 'I—he's a nice man, but—my mother was his sister, you see, and he thinks I'm a *responsibility*. I don't want to live where I'm just a responsibility. He's—he's busy, and works hard, and goes places where I can't go, and he never stops to play with me, or anything—but he does send me to a private school.'

'I see. He takes his responsibility seriously, though?'

'Yes, ma'am.'

The judge thought for a moment. 'You leave us with a difficult situation, Robbie,' she finally sighed. 'You don't want to live with your father, and you don't want to live with your mother—by adoption,' the judge hastily qualified as the boy stirred into objection. 'Do you have any ideas?'

'Sure,' the boy proclaimed. 'I've got a perfect solution. I wanna—excuse me—I want to live with Phil.'

A deadly silence fell over the entire room. 'And who the devil is Phil?' The judge leaned forward over her desk to stare at the boy. Philomena shrugged her shoulders. After all, they had outlawed the death penalty. So what else could happen to her? She stood up, still clutching at Robbie's hand.

'I'm Phil,' she announced in her soft ready-for-battle voice.

'And I wanna stay with Phil because she wants me,' the boy interjected swiftly. 'She doesn't have any responsibility—about me, that is, and she doesn't want my money—she just wants me. And that's what I want. I want somebody who wants me.' And with that he slumped back in his chair, pulling Phil down with him, clutching at her hand as if defying the world to separate them.

'Now let me see if I've got this right,' the judge sighed. 'This woman is cohabiting with Mr Wilderman, and you want her to be your legal guardian?' From behind, the lawyer nudged Phil sharply. She turned around. He gestured towards her left hand.

'Your honour,' she offered tentatively. 'If you mean I'm living with Penn and that's a bad thing, it's not, you know. It's really very nice.' Chuckles surrounded her. 'I forgot to tell you my full name. I'm Philomena Peabody Wilderman. Penn and I are married, and I think Robbie should live with us—because—because Penn is the nicest man I've ever known, and it takes two parents to bring up a teenager, and I know because I've had lots of experience in that field, and so—I think Robbie should go home with us.' And she collapsed into her chair again, and tried to shrink into a smaller package than she was. Another hand trapped her, on her left side. She was thoroughly surrounded. Penn on one side, holding her gently; Robbie on the other, clutching desperately, so that her hand ached.

The judge looked at all of them, one at a time, counting, assessing. And finally she tapped on her desk a couple of times with the top of her pen. 'I think maybe you're right,' she finally said. 'So ordered.' That pen again, an extra rap, and the judge billowed out of the courtroom, followed by her marching legion.

Luckily the room had two separate exits, or there might have been blood on the sand after all, Phil thought.

'I'll appeal!' Eloise yelled after them, as half her lawyer-platoon held her from making a frontal assault. 'I'll appeal!' They could still hear it echoing down the hall as they headed for the stairs.

Robbie was still clutching her hand, and it ached so much that she finally could not suppress a whimper. Penn turned around in a flash. He had been walking ahead of them, his arm on his lawyer's.

'It's only my hand,' she said quickly. 'Robbie doesn't know his own strength.'

'Gee, you should have said something,' the boy returned, releasing the pressure. 'Oh, what a mess I made!'

'It's not a mess,' she assured him. 'It just needs a massage and a——'

She stopped in mid-sentence. Penn had turned away and was going down the stairs. She could read anger in the set of his shoulders. It was still there when she followed him into the back seat of the limousine. Robbie—a smiling Robbie—jumped into the front seat, and was quickly lost in conversation with Harry—about machinery, of course. Phil settled back into the seat, and made an attempt to lift up the arm-rest. Penn's heavy hand kept her from doing so.

'So don't bottle it all up,' she said quietly. 'Whatever it is, it belongs out in the open. You won the case. Robbie is yours.'

'No,' he said bitterly. 'I didn't win the case, and Robbie isn't mine.'

'Penn! What are you trying to say?'

'I'm trying to tell you the truth,' he muttered. 'I didn't win the case. You did. The judge didn't appoint *me* to be the boy's guardian, she appointed *you*. And in any case, you were right a week or so ago. You said he hated me, and obviously he does.'

'He doesn't hate you, Penn. He defended you in the court. He laughed with you, and——'

'And he also told the absolute truth,' her husband grated. 'All I ever did was put a roof over his head and feed him. Nothing more. I was always too busy—too wrapped up in the Big World. I kept him away from the river because I remembered how his mother died. I couldn't go with him, so no Little League. No Boy Scouts. With the finest mountains in the world within forty miles of us, I've never once taken him camping. It's all damn true, but it took you to bring it all out, Peabody. Sometimes I'm not sure whether meeting you was good or bad for me.'

The bitterness was more than she had expected. She tried to defend herself. '*I* didn't win the case,' she sighed. 'The judge misunderstood. I was speaking for you!'

'I know that,' he grunted. 'Maybe I could have better spoken for myself!'

It was a cold, flat statement. For the past few minutes she had been hugging herself, congratulating herself, and now suddenly it all exploded in her face. He settled back in his seat, a frown on his handsome face. She studied him. He had the look of a man troubled beyond his capacity. And then, just as suddenly, his muscles relaxed, the frown disappeared. One of his warm hands fumbled for hers, squeezed it gently, and held on to it as the car moved out into traffic on the way home.

'It's not your fault, Philomena,' he sighed. 'It just seemed for a moment that—well, it's one problem out of our way.'

'But your—but Eloise—she said they would appeal.'

'So let them,' he said wryly. 'I can afford to hire more lawyers than that damn St Louis wimp. We'll lead them a merry chase before they get *that* decision overturned. You did a good job, old girl!' Congratulations, but the taste was bittersweet.

How can I be so high up in the air on one side, and so low down on the other, she asked herself. Congratulations—old girl. Darn. I *should* have told him the first time the subject came up. And now I don't know *what* to do! She was still deep in thought when the car drew up at the front door.

CHAPTER NINE

THE atmosphere of tension was still there when she came down to dinner. Robbie appeared with clean face and hands, and something that might be called a smile on his face. Harry was his usually glum self, and Penn had withdrawn somewhere inside that darkness of his, and no amount of conversation would bring him out. After the meal Harry guided him into the library, and before the door closed behind them she could hear the hum of conversation.

'So that leaves you and me, Robbie,' Phil offered tentatively. 'Or have you got something on too?'

The boy shrugged his shoulders. 'I was going to watch *Dr Who* on television, but if you and—Dad—I thought both of you would like to be alone for a while, so——'

'No, don't disturb your plans,' she returned hastily. 'I've got a million things to do. You just go ahead.'

He proffered a real smile this time, and when he walked by her chair he stopped long enough to kiss her cheek. 'It takes some getting used to,' he said, 'but maybe I could like having a real mother around the place.'

'Well, don't get over-enthusiastic,' she returned. 'Who knows? Given enough time I might be able to put up with you.' She reached up, ruffled his hair, and giggled.

'You don't plan to disappear now, do you?'

'It all depends on how you mean that,' she said. 'I *do* intend to disappear. Out into the garden, before it gets dark. Run along, kid.'

It was still light outside, in those minutes after the sun

had gone but before the dark had taken over. She wandered slowly down into the garden, towards the hot house. Mr Yu was still working inside, and she was in no mood for casual chatter. She turned back and sat down on the sofa-swing. The tip of her toe barely reached the ground. The whole construction was adapted for long-legged men, she accused. Two blue jays refused to accept her comment, and fled, flying low over the shrubbery in the direction of the park. In the background she could hear Mr Yu singing. She braced herself and gave the swing a shove, then coiled her legs up beneath her and tried to relax.

Being a wife, if only a temporary one, was proving more nerve-racking than she had thought. His offer had puzzled her as much as her own acceptance—until that moment on the steps of the church. But the fact that she loved him was no guarantee that he felt the same. Something temporary, he had said. Until the problem with Robbie was disposed of, and he gets his sight back. Well, Robbie was—settled, not disposed of. And on Monday morning the doctor would remove his pads for the final time. And then what?

Her mind balked at the jump, and left her wandering around in her head as the gold on the western horizon began to fade into the blue and purple that heralded the end of day. Although she was in the centre of the city the trees and purposefully curved streets cut out the traffic noises, and left only a certain empty tranquillity on her ears. The swing squeaked a little as she lowered a foot and gave another push. Mr Yu's song had a haunting familiarity about it, but the name escaped her. She nestled back in the corner of the swing, and wrestled with her devils again.

'Mrs Wilderman?' Harry, standing on the little ridge

that overlooked the pool area. Just a shadow now.

'Here,' she answered softly. The little man sidled down the hillside in a rush of gravel.

Mrs Wilderman? What a nice sound. She had heard it so seldom these last two days. 'What is it, Harry?'

'I have to go now.'

'I—what?' Harry was a part of the family. A fixture in the house. Every minute of every day, where Penn was, there was Harry. It was almost impossible to think of Harry as having to 'go now'! She dropped her foot to the ground and braked the swing to a stop. 'You have to *go*?'

'A ten o'clock flight,' he returned.

'But you—how the devil can Penn get around if you——?'

'He has you now.'

An overwhelming statement. He has *me* now. If only it were true! 'I—I don't understand, Harry.'

'It's simple enough. I have to make a trip. I'll be gone two or three days—well, to be exact I expect to get things wound up by Sunday. But my plane leaves in a couple of hours, and he needs you now.'

'I—yes. Yes, of course, Harry. Where is he?'

'In the living-room.'

'I'll go in at once. And Harry?'

'What?'

'Have a safe trip.'

The little man had disappeared before she could gather her wits about her. Mr Yu was making closing-for-the-night noises down in the greenhouse. And Penn was waiting for her? She jumped up, setting the swing into a wild creaking and groaning. The gravel of the path crunched under her sandals as she made her way back up to the house.

The house was quiet, as if it had gone to sleep. Penn

was sitting on the big couch in the middle of the room,
facing the door. Somehow he sensed her. She stopped to
scan his face, uplifted in her direction. There was
something dear about it, something heartwarming. She
floated over the distance between them. He was holding
out a hand. She took it, and followed his direction as he
tugged her down to sit beside him.

'Well, Mrs Wilderman.' The second time in one night!
She pinched herself, just to make sure, and then settled
back. His arm automatically came around her shoulders.

'Well, Mr Wilderman?' she sighed.

'What we need now is a nice fire in the fireplace.'

'Yes.' She snuggled closer to him. 'What fireplace?'

'The one right in front of us.'

'That's a door,' she offered.

'You need more imagination,' he returned. 'A big
stone fireplace. And the flames? They're blue on the top,
a flickering blue.'

'Silly. It's still a door. A double door, I grant you, but
there aren't any blue flames.'

'Pragmatic Philomena?'

A deep-throated chuckle. 'The girls called me Practical Pill.'

'Pill?'

'Well, it was hard to say Philomena when they were
young, and then when they got older, they thought Pill
was more appropriate.'

'Tell me about them.'

So she did, emphasising the good, making herself the
butt of the bad, not knowing how clearly she silhouetted
her own loneliness, demonstrating how quickly her youth
had fled. 'And now it's your turn,' she concluded.

'Not much to tell,' he assured her. 'Compared to you
I'm practically a stay-at-home. Although they did call me

the "Wild Man" when I was younger. A dare-devil fool, that's what my father called me. Up until——'

'Until your sister's accident?'

'Ah. You know about that too?'

'Kitchen gossip,' she said, feeling a compassion for him that went beyond all bonds.

'She never would have gone out on the river if I hadn't teased and dared her. Never could let things alone. She always had to do everything big brother did. And the race was the most stupid thing imaginable. There was debris in the chanel. She must have been going ninety miles an hour when her boat hit the floating tree trunk. It threw them both almost a hundred feet. They were both dead before—well—it was all my fault, and the cloud has hung over me ever since. If only I could have that little time to live over again.'

'And that's what drives Penn Wilderman?'

He crushed her against him with one strong arm. She could feel his fingers sink into her shoulder. 'And that's what drives Penn Wilderman,' he said bitterly. 'I'd better get to bed.'

His hand relaxed. Phil rubbed her shoulder where the fingers had dug craters, and then stood up. As soon as he heard her move, he came up too. Holding his hand, she guided him up the stairs and into his own bedroom. Still holding her, he took himself to the big armchair next to the bed, and sat down.

'Eyedrops,' she offered, trying to get a little normality into her voice.

'Yes, please. Not many more times to go,' he answered. 'Lord, doesn't that sound good?'

She dimmed the overhead lights, found the drops on his dresser, and administered them. 'Hey, what's the hurry?' he grumbled. 'No sooner do you get the pads off than you flood me. I wanted to get a look at you.'

And that's just what I *don't* want, she told herself.
We've gone this far in the dark, and I want to keep it that
way until the last possible minute! 'Don't touch those
pads,' she warned. 'It's just a few days before the grand
unveiling, and all will be revealed!'

'You make it sound like a Hallowe'en project,' he
complained.

'Well, this is no time to ruin weeks of work,' she told
him. 'Be optimistic, Penn.'

'Oh, I am,' he returned. There was just a touch of
sarcasm, just a touch of despair. 'But have you ever
thought—suppose I go down to the doctor on Monday, in
all my darkness, and he takes the pads off—and the
world is still dark?'

'It won't happen,' she assured him. 'I just *know*
everything will be OK. Here are your pyjamas, at the foot
of the bed. I have to check up on Robbie.'

'Damn that kid,' he said. 'You married me, not
Robbie.'

'I know, but he needs somebody to——'

'So do I,' he snarled at her. 'Go ahead!'

The depth of his anger reached her. She reacted by
running. None of her experience had taught her how to
deal with an angry husband. But kids——

So Robbie, still following a horror movie on Channel
Six, was quickly disabused of the notion that his sweet
lovable mother would let him sit up until midnight. She
hustled the boy into the shower, picked up the clothes he
had strewn across the floor, and went back to her own
room.

An hour later, bathed, perfumed, but not yet calm, she
stood by her window. Her translucent pink nightgown,
the one that reached her ankles, but hung loosely at her

shoulders on two shoe-string bands, flared around her.
Half dreaming, she watched the star patterns. There was
a noise from next door, a strangled cough.

Surely Penn must be asleep by now, she told herself,
but could not stop the movement that carried her through
the connecting door into his bedroom. Penn was in bed,
apparently asleep, but the lights were still on. And *his*
clothes were strewn around the room. He has an excuse,
she told herself fiercely as she bent to the task, and then
laid out the clean things he would need in the morning.

He stirred in the bed as she finished. She froze in
position, sure that her vague movements, her mutterings,
might have awakened him. When he became quiet again
she edged cautiously over to the door and flicked off the
light switch. The change from light to dark blinded her.
She blinked her eyes, holding fast until some of the
darkness became less dark, some of the shadows became
more distinct. Gently, she whispered across the rug
towards her own room, then stopped and came back to
kneel beside him. Her gentle hands brushed the lock of
hair back from his forehead, and offered a loving kiss.
And before she could move both his hands snatched at
her.

'Gotcha,' he whispered, pulling her closer.

'Darn you, I thought you were asleep! I——'

'I wanted to see you.'

'I'm not going to have you take those pads off your
eyes,' she stormed at him. 'You're worse than Robbie is,
for goodness' sake!'

'I don't need to see you with my eyes,' he contradicted.
'Be still.' It was a command she could not refuse. She
didn't want to refuse. His hands had given up their
imperious grip on her upper arms, and were now shaping
her face, running through the softness of her long hair.

She knelt there beside the bed, ignoring the complaints from her leg muscles. Hardly receiving them, for a fact. All the lines of communication to her brain were tied up in the sensual assault those hands were making as they dropped gently down on to her shoulders, pushed the straps of her nightgown away, and coursed down on to the proud pulsing mounds of her aroused breasts. Somewhere in the distance she could hear the hiss of his breath as he caressed and measured the fullness of her, the proud upward tilting of her womanhood.

One of his hands slipped downwards brushing the gown off her hips, as it explored the softness of her rib cage, the sharp inward curve of her waist, the burgeoning outward bulge of her full hip. And then back upwards again, to torture her breast.

Madness raced through her mind as she fought herself. One half of her screamed for more. The other half kept at a litany. *It's only a temporary marriage. It's only temporary!* There was little doubt which half might win—until he laughed. 'No doubt about it, old girl,' he commented, 'You are a whole lot of woman.'

'No doubt,' she whispered bitterly as she scrambled away from the bed and restored her nightgown. Dear old girl. There's nothing special about *this* man, she told herself. He's just like all the others. All cats look grey on a dark night! Damn him! It was hard to lock in the whimper of anger and frustration.

He sat up in the bed. She could see the shadows moving, and took another step backwards. 'I didn't mean to make you cry,' he said sombrely. 'Come back here.'

'Well, you managed to, no matter what you meant!' She retreated into her own room and slammed the door behind her. It wasn't *all* his fault, her conscience

proclaimed. Maybe not, she thought angrily, but if I
don't blame *him*, I have to blame myself—and I don't
want to do that! Wearily she stumbled across the room in
the dark and flung herself down on the bed.

It was a wasted effort. She tossed and turned all night,
but sleep would not come. When the fingers of dawn light
touched on the trees outside she gave it all up, went for a
quick shower, and hastily crammed herself into fresh
underwear, a pair of old dungarees and a T-shirt. Rose
and the maids were off on vacation. Harry had gone.
Frank lived out in an apartment over the garage, and Mr
Yu would be coming in. The old man would make the
dinner, but breakfast and lunch were in her hands.
Make-up was not worth the effort, but she did take time
to brush out her hair before she went down to the
kitchen.

The only solution, she decided, was to keep her fingers
busy and her mind empty. She scavenged up utensils,
broke half a dozen eggs, and scrambled them. Sausages
went into the microwave. Bread went into the toaster.
The coffee pot began to bubble. She scattered a few
plates on the huge kitchen table, added coffee mugs, and
plodded determinedly back up the stairs to serve as
Penn's guide. He hardly seemed to need one. She went
into the room and closed the door behind her. He was just
coming back into the room, followed by a spiral of steam
from his shower. He was using his towel to scrub at his
unruly hair.

It was a sight she had never seen before. The dominant
male, in all his naked glory. A week ago she would have
screamed and run. Today she stood with her back against
the door, trying to breathe so softly that he could not
hear. And admired. He was every bit as male as she was
female. Sleek, muscular, broad shouldered, narrow hips.

Strong heavy thighs—and everything else, beautifully proportioned. He fumbled for a moment at his clothing, and she almost broke away from the door to help. Almost. His groping hands found everything where she had placed it the night before. Very slowly, it seemed, he balanced on one leg at a time and struggled into his shorts. Slacks followed, and then a sports shirt.

She was congratulating herself on not being discovered as he bent to lace up his shoes. 'Enjoy the show, did you?' he asked casually. He stood up and brushed at his slacks as he turned directly toward her. Startled, she looked at his eyes. The pads were still in place.

'Damn you,' she muttered.

'The door squeaks,' he told her as he started to move towards the sound of her voice. 'See everything you wanted?'

He was within reach at that moment. Her hand seemed to move involuntarily. It jumped to his forehead, and her fingers combed through his hair, smoothing and shaping it. 'That's nice,' he said. 'We must do this more often.'

There was just enough sarcasm in his voice to bring her back to reality. She snapped her hand back. Her finger tips were burning. 'I suppose you've come to take me to breakfast?'

'Damn you,' she sighed. His hand dropped on her shoulder. She turned, opened the door, and led him out into the hall and down the stairs. Robbie clattered up behind them, half shouting a greeting, passed them on the stairs, and hesitated just long enough to give his 'new' mother a light kiss. He was gone into the kitchen before the pair of them reached the bottom step.

'Damn kid,' Penn commented. She almost jumped, startled by his first words outside the bedroom.

'Don't talk like that,' she retorted fiercely. 'He's a sensitive boy—and both words are operative.'

'Me too,' he chuckled. 'I'm a sensitive boy too. And he's stealing my act.'

'I don't know what you mean,' she snapped. He demonstrated. But his kiss wasn't aimed at her cheek, and in no way could it be called fleeting. When they both came through the kitchen door Robbie, who was half-way through the scrambled eggs, laughed like a fool.

She guided Penn over to his chair, and then glared at the boy. 'What are you laughing at, you——' She stamped her foot on the hard floor, too late to remember she had no shoes on.

'You and Dad,' the boy chuckled through another mouthful of food. 'You don't *hafta* hide in the hall to get kissed. I know all about that stuff. Why is your face so red, Phil?'

'Because you don't know all you think you know,' she snarled. 'And there's nothing I hate worse than cheerful people in the morning! Leave your father some sausages!'

Robbie and Penn spent most of the morning together in his library. Conspiring about something, Phil thought as she rushed through a brief dusting and rearranging, and then went upstairs. I'm angry. Why? At whom? And had no answer.

Robbie had heard the 'cleanliness' message. His room was as neat as a new pin, bed made up, magazines put away, clothes on hangers. And we'll see how long that lasts, Phil snorted, as she made her way down the hall to Penn's room. Everything was as it had been earlier— except that that magnificent body was missing. She picked up the wet towel. It was a crazy thing to do, but she rubbed it gently against her cheek before dropping it

into the clothes hamper. His pyjamas were still huddled
up at the foot of the bed, unused. She re-folded them and
put them back in the drawer. And then the bed.

It was a very difficult bed to make. Not that it was
over-large, oddly formed. Every time her hand reached
for a pillow or a sheet or a blanket it just seemed to linger,
as if some sustenance could be drawn from its emptiness.
'Come on, girl,' she told herself. 'You're going down with
something. Get to work.' It might have taken something
more than words—horse whips, perhaps—but a thump
of feet on the stairs served instead. She finished making
up the bed in twenty seconds flat, and ran for her own
room. She spent the rest of the day trying to avoid
everyone else who lived in the house. And since they all
suddenly appeared to be very busy, it wasn't too hard a
job.

Saturday night Robbie served as his father's guide.
Phil could hear them from her hiding-place next door.
There was considerable laughter. It served to warm up a
very tiny portion of her chilled heart. For all the
muddling, all the interference, all the upset she had
caused, at least one good thing had resulted. Robbie and
his father had come to appreciate each other.

Exhausted from a sleepless night and a fugitive day,
Phil went to bed early, slept the sleep of the just, and
awakened to a household already in motion. She could
hear multiple thumps up and down the stairs, banging
noises from the area of the kitchen, and motor noises
from a car at the front door. She checked her bedside
clock. Seven o'clock. Sunday morning? It seemed
impossible. She threw back the covers, snatched at her
heavy blue robe, and cautiously peered into Penn's room.
Empty.

Through his room, just in case, and out into the hall.

Empty. Down the stairs and into the kitchen. Robbie was stuffing his face with buttered toast. His father, fully dressed, across the table from him, was deep in thought. Harry was back, standing by the sink, a big smile on his face.

'Tarpon?' the boy asked through a mouthful of bread.

'Bonito,' Harry returned. 'Everything.'

Robbie looked up just in time to catch Phil standing in the door. 'Isn't it great, Mom?' he cried.

The two adults turned in her direction. 'Yes,' she managed. 'It's great. What?'

'Fishing,' Robbie said. 'Dad's arranged for me to go down to Catalina for a week of deep-sea fishing! Harry's coming with me, and we'll camp out on the boat and—wow!'

'Wow indeed. You'll need more breakfast than that.'

'I can't wait. The plane leaves at eight o'clock. We've only an hour to get to the airport, but I'm all packed, and—Mom? Didn't anybody tell you?'

'No, I guess not.' Phil tried to sound cheerful. It was bad enough to have to smile at seven o'clock on a Sunday morning, but—no, nobody had told her, had hinted, had even suggested. Tomorrow his father comes out from under the bandages. Today we ship Harry and Robbie off for a week of deep-sea fishing. Mr Yu is too old to travel but lives in his own little house out at the back. Frank is required to take Penn to the doctor's. And that leaves only me, she thought. What about me?

But none of her agitation showed in her voice. 'No, that's OK,' she told the boy. 'I get seasick just thinking about water. A whole week. I'll bet you'll have fun.' She slipped into the chair between her two 'men' and snatched at the last piece of toast on the plate. Harry thumped a mug of black coffee down in front of her.

'Yeah, well, women have that kind of trouble,' Robbie pontificated from the depths of his thirteen years of experience with life. 'Only—I wish Dad were coming. But of course, with his eyes and all—next time, Dad?'

'Next time, Robbie.' It was the first time Penn had spoken, and it didn't sound all that enthusiastic—or is it something else, Phil asked herself. She was straining, these days, to register nuances—to read behind the words. And there was definitely something there to be read.

'We gotta go,' Harry contributed. 'All the stuff's in the car. Come on, kid.'

The car was moving before Phil could get to the front door. She waved a belated goodbye to the back of the vehicle, and was rewarded when Robbie stuck his head out the window and blew her a kiss.

Penn was still at table, nursing his coffee-mug, a dour look on his face. Phil plumped herself down in the nearest chair and pulled her mug over in front of her. The coffee had cooled just about to the edge of drinkability. 'It'll be all right,' she said softly. 'He'll enjoy every minute of it. And he will be safe, won't he?'

'He'll be safe,' he returned gruffly. 'Happy, I don't know. Safe, I'm sure of.'

'So what brought all this on so suddenly?' She leaned both elbows on the table, the coffee-mug treasured between her hands. Penn was wearing that office mask, a look of non-committal interest that gave nothing away. His fingers were drumming on the table-top. She remembered where they last had drummed, and blushed. 'Is there something wrong, Penn?'

'Wrong? How the hell could there be anything wrong?' he roared at her. His chair fell over as he moved violently away from the table. 'I'm going back upstairs. You

needn't come. When Frank comes back from the airport
send him up to see me.' He stomped out.

She heard him stumble on the stairs, and repressed the
urge to run after him. Somehow or another, she knew, he
was not prepared to accept any help from her this day.
This is strange, she told herself as she started to clean up
the kitchen. Sometimes I feel very married, and
sometimes I feel—like a stranger in their midst.

It was another sunny day—the first day of March, for a
fact. Spring was hustling about in the valley where the
American and the Sacramento rivers met. She snapped
on the kitchen radio as she worked. Ski-ing conditions
were still perfect up in the mountains, forty miles away,
with deep-packed snow. She stretched up on tiptoe to
look out of the small kitchen window. Mr Yu was
transplanting flowers out of his greenhouse into the beds
in the back garden. In the middle of the garden a pair of
robins were strutting. She felt the need to share, dropped
the rest of the dishes hastily into the dishwasher, and
dashed upstairs to dress.

She wandered around the gardens all the remainder of
the morning, and then went back in, having promised
Mr Yu that she would see to the evening meal. The house
was like a tomb.

As she headed for the kitchen Frank came out of the
living-room and started for the front door. 'He's in the
library,' he said in passing. 'He tells me to get out and
take the rest of the day off. You be OK?'

'Me? Oh, yes.' Just to be sure, after Frank had left Phil
went along to the library and cracked the door slightly
open, just enough to see her husband sitting at his desk, a
glass paperweight in his hands, and an almost-lost look
on his face. As gently as she knew how, she closed the

door and went back out into the kitchen.

They shared dinner in the kitchen. 'It's not worth carrying everything to the dining-room just for the two of us,' he said when she went to get him. He looked tired, as if all the little tensions had become one big one. There was no discussion at the table. He ate the Western omelette she put in front of him, drank the coffee, enjoyed a slice of the apple pie, and said nothing.

An hour later, having stood the silence as long as she could, she got up and started on the dishes. It was growing dark outside. She took a quick look. Thunderclouds obscured the setting sun. She could hear the boom and rumble in the distance, as the storm did its work.

'It looks like a bad storm,' she commented. 'I think I'll have to put the lights on.'

'Yeah, you do that,' he said bitterly. 'At least one of us might as well be in the light.'

'Oh Penn,' she sighed. 'Please. It will all be over tomorrow. You'll see.'

'You're damn well right,' he returned. 'Everything will be over tomorrow. I'm going upstairs.' Fighting the chill in her heart, Phil came around the table and offered her hand. He brushed it aside. 'I don't need any guide dogs,' he grumbled as he pushed back his chair and felt his way along the wall to the door. 'Just keep out of my way.'

She collapsed in a chair. It was worse than she had ever expected. *Just keep out of my way! Tomorrow it will all be over!* Her head ached, as if the storm had shifted to the inside of her head. 'Oh, Penn,' she moaned as she dropped her head into her arms on the table. The tears that followed upset her more than anything else. Practical Philomena just didn't cry. The world was too full of things to be done. There was no room for crybabies. She knuckled the last drop of water from her eyes, and marched out into the living-room.

By nine-thirty she had read the same page of her novel over for the twentieth time, her headache had abated slightly, and she hadn't heard a sound in the house since seven o'clock. 'Well, there's no use struggling,' she lectured herself. 'Staying up late won't put off tomorrow. It's going to be, come hell or high water.'

Phil got up, stretched mightily, and then performed the nightly ritual, going around the house, locking windows and doors, and setting the burglar alarm. It was something that Harry usually did—and just the doing of it reminded her that Harry and Robbie were far away. Another little stab in her heart, that. If Robbie were at home perhaps they might have talked together—played games—built up some camaraderie? She turned off all but the night lights, and went upstairs slowly, feeling like some old hag whose days were numbered. There was no sound from Penn's room. The thunder was still working its way around the basin of the valley, and rain was thundering for admission. Not one to be plagued by storms, she felt something different in this one. Some evil, trying to reach out and pluck her from the safety of her home.

She closed her door behind her, then trailed clothes across the floor—doing just what she hated most when Robbie did it. By the time she reached the bathroom she had completely stripped.

The hot water revived her. Shower cap tucked tightly around her mass of hair, she revelled in the beat of the water on her skin. The sounds of the shower shut out the storm—and everything else. The soap felt sensuous as she lathered her hands and rubbed them up and down her body—and dreamed. If it could be Penn's hands? Penn's arms? Too much to hope for. She reached for the cold water and smashed the dream to bits under an icy deluge.

The bath towels were immense. She used one to dry herself, then wrapped the other around her, sarong-fashion. Her hair was dripping at its ends, where the shower cap had failed its mission. A little brushing, she assured herself, and walked out into the dark bedroom. There was someone there. Penn. Standing by the windows, listening to the rush of water against the panes.

'Penn? You wanted something?'

'My eyedrops.'

'Oh! I thought you said yesterday that you wouldn't want another——'

'Well, I do.' How could everything that seemed so warm and loving turn into such coldness, she asked herself. Have I done anything to deserve all that?

'All right,' she returned, using her softest voice. 'Sit on the bed here, and——'

Whatever it was he wanted, it wasn't eyedrops. He seized her proffered hand and yanked her up against him. She backed away and he followed. Backed until the inside of her knees banged into the side of the bed. 'What—I don't understand,' she managed. 'What do you want, Penn? Have you been drinking?'

'Not a drop. You don't really understand, Philomena? I'm your husband, and it's dark inside here. I want a little comfort.'

'Inside? You want me to put on a light?'

'I want you to *be* a light, Philomena!' He pushed. Trapped against the bed, she fell over backwards and suddenly he was on top of her.

'What—Penn!' The towel was gone. Ripped away and discarded over his shoulder. His robe followed. 'Penn!' Not a scream, but a soft reproach. 'I didn't expect this. It wasn't part of our——'

'Bargain? This is a marriage, not a bargain. Did you expect I could lie there next door to you and never have an inclination?'

'Is that what it is, Penn? Just an inclination? You need someone to pick on, and I'm the nearest? Is that why you sent Robbie and Harry away?' It was getting harder to talk, to reason, than she had ever supposed. His hands were roving over her face, along the line of her neck, down to her breasts. His weight was no longer a burden, but some sort of promise. That's all you need do, she told herself fiercely. Talk to him, be calm, keep cool. But her traitorous body wanted nothing of the kind.

She could hardly suppress the moan as his hands shifted lower, to her hips and below, and his lips took their place at her breast. The breath blew out of her as wild spasms shot through her nervous system, and reported in to her brain. So many feelings, so many reports, that her control centre was at the point of overload.

'Don't. Please, Penn—don't.' A weak effort—her strained voice trying to give one answer while her rolling hips gave another. His hands stopped.

'You don't want this?'

'I—no!' That last word took all her remaining control.

'Then fight me off,' he snarled.

She was fully stretched out, her nerves jangling, perspiration pouring from her, her legs spread. 'I won't fight you,' she sighed. 'I can't. But it isn't part of our bargain *or* our marriage, Penn.' The hands started moving again, his lips followed. Not a mad physical assault, but a teasing that drew her out from herself, sent her tossing and turning out of control.

'You don't want me to do this?' A hiss out of the darkness. Her eyes were shut tight. She could not muster

an answer, but her tossing, squirming body told him all
he wanted to know. Those lips teased at her, nibbling her
ear-lobes, running channels of fire down to her breasts,
across her stomach, until she could stand no more. Her
hands snatched at his hair. He hesitated for a moment in
his wild pursuit. But instead of pushing him away she
pulled him closer, hard against the softness of her. Her
mouth was half open. It was hard to breathe. When he
came into her it was like a benison.

There was a sharp momentary pain, hidden quickly in
the glory that followed, as their wild passion drove them
up to and over the edge. She screamed at the joy of it,
wrapping arms and legs around him, refusing to let him
go. After that one last surge he was strangely quiet, his
hands holding his weight up off her. The fever in her
mind gradually subsided, until she recognised the real
world. *So that's what it's all about, she told herself. How
wonderful!* She felt a tiny chill as air moved across her wet
skin. *What wonders marriage can bring. I love him more
than ever.* The glory of it filled her. And then he spoiled
everything.

He rolled away from her and sat up on the edge of the
bed, holding his head. 'Penn?' she queried. 'It was——'

'I didn't mean that to happen, Philomena,' he groaned.
'I didn't expect that you would still be a virgin—not at
your age. I—I'm sorry. I'll try to make it up to you.'

She sat up carefully behind him, feeling the ache in her
bones and muscles, feeling the despair sweeping over
her. It was all a mistake, that's what he's telling me now?
He may have wanted *it*, but he doesn't want *me*. Oh,
God!

'Make what up to me?' Her voice was like glass, ready
to shatter at any moment.

'All of that,' he returned. 'I don't even know what to call it.'

The glory had gone out of life. She felt as deep in blackness as he must, behind those terrible pads. He wanted a woman, she told herself fiercely, and I'm the only one available! 'The word they commonly use is rape,' she said, and the bitterness rolled off her tongue, poisoning every word. 'Rape,' she threw after him as he stumbled off in the darkness to his own room. 'Rape,' she whispered against the door that he slammed behind him. It wasn't rape, and she knew it without question. Seduction, yes, but not rape. She was trying to hurt him with words as much as he had hurt her. He had turned all that beauty, all that wonderful experience, into something that animals do, without feeling. Something precious had died in that dark room. She wept for it.

CHAPTER TEN

DESPITE the agonies, the tears, the recriminations, Phil finally fell asleep, and when she awakened the California sun was bright in the sky. She sat up quickly. The room and bed showed the ravages of the previous night. Her bedside clock reported ten in the morning. All she could think of was Penn. This was the morning he was to have his eye pads removed. She had to be gone before he came back. The idea rolled over and over in her troubled mind. She had married him to help keep Robbie in Sacramento, and that task had been accomplished. He had always said it would be a short marriage—a temporary device. But she had not counted on falling in love with him!

And last night, wasn't that the confirmation? He had taken her to emotional peaks of which she had never dreamed, and then cruelly dumped her off the mountain. She dressed hurriedly. Slacks and sweater, her long curls tied back carelessly into a pony-tail, and low-heeled shoes. A few personal items crammed into a case. Leave the rest, but hurry! Down the stairs for the last time, pausing to salute the Pirate and squeezing out one last tear for the Lady. Steal by the kitchen door. Rose is at work, singing at the top of her lungs. Hurry.

No time for goodbyes. Robbie would just have to understand. Out of the door into the sunshine, around the house to the garage. Her little car, shining like new, started immediately. As soon as the engine settled into a regular beat she drove around the house to the front door.

Up the stairs, into the hall, where her suitcase waited. Back to the door—too late. She could hear the imperious purr of the Cadillac as it swept around the drive and halted just behind her own car. Too late. Her hand moved towards the doorknob, but before she could grip it, the door flew open. Penn.

He stood in the doorway, staring at her. The pads were gone. A pair of dark sunglasses covered eyes that could definitely see. Eyes that followed her as she shrank against the left wall, out of his reach, out of his way. He had that facial expression that one sees on the statues of Caesars—autocratic, commanding, solemn.

'You can see again,' she managed to whisper.

'Who the hell are you?' he snapped. He took off the glasses. Dark brown, almost black eyes searched her up and down. 'What's going on?' he snarled. 'I know you, but——' Some thought snatched his attention away, he strode down the hall and started up the stairs. She heard him stop, half-way up.

It was worse than she had expected. 'Who the hell are you?' I guess that's a great way to sum up a marriage, she gibbered to herself as she grabbed the suitcase and ran. She was in the car, engine running, when he came back to the door. 'Hey, you!' he yelled. The old car jumped as she jammed it into gear. Gravel spurted as the wheels spun. She accelerated down the drive, one eye on her rear-view mirror. He came down the stairs, hastily restored the dark glasses to the bridge of his nose, and watched, hands on hips as she turned left and disappeared from sight.

Traffic was heavy, as it was every Monday morning in the centre of the city. Phil found it hard to concentrate.

'Running away from your husband.' The phrase kept repeating itself, pounding in her ears like a dirge. 'Yes,' she yelled to the world at large, 'and if he catches me——' And then she came to her senses. What do you mean, *if he catches me*? Whatever gives you the idea that he is even going to try? You know where you rate, Philomena. But just in case!

Just in case, she swung the wheel hard left on P Street, heading westward towards the river. The parking lot at Pacific Mines and Metals seemed full. She pulled up in front of the building and parked in the No Parking zone. A guard came out of the building, waving his hand, and came to a full stop when he saw who she was.

'Good morning, Mrs Wilderman. Will you be here long?' Listen to the anxiety, she told herself grimly as she powered past him into the building. He's helping me break the law, and doesn't dare do otherwise because of Penn. If it were not for Penn, he would have thrown me in the river and had my car towed away. The idea made her angry, and anger overcame fright. She stalked into the typing pool as if she were a queen. All the noises stopped. She gave them all a vacant smile, a quick wave, and slid into one of the empty booths. Her fingers were slippery with perspiration. Phil wiped them off on her slacks, punched up the computer terminal, entered the Personnel Access Code, and sat back as the computer unrolled all the names of employees starting with the letter P. P for Peabody. She slapped at the stop key.

And there I am, she snarled at herself. One entry in a thousand. Peabody, Philomena Mary. File Number 621. Address and telephone number. Date of first employment. Pay increases. Promotions. Commendations. Health record, next of kin. Ten years of work, all summarised in green on the display panel. She glared at it, doing her best to hold back the tears. You can't drive in California while crying, she told herself. It's against the law.

'Phil?' She looked up over her shoulder. Harriet, the new supervisor, stood there, and the last thing I need, Phil told herself, is a long conversation—or someone looking over my shoulder to see what I'm doing. The screen glittered at her as the electronic circuits waited for further instructions. Her hand moved to the keyboard and typed Peabody, Philomena Mary, File Number 621. ERASE. She slapped down hard on the command. The computer ruminated for a second, then flashed a message: 'Are you sure?' She dragged her hand back for just a second and typed 'Yes'. *Peabody Philomena Mary*, glared at her for a second, then disappeared from sight and from memory. Just to be sure, when the computer displayed the query sign she ordered it to search for Peabody, Philomena Mary, File Number 621. The machine grumbled for a second, then reported 'No such file exists'. Now—he'll never find me, she told herself as she turned off the terminal and struggled to her feet. *If he ever wants to!*

'Have to hurry,' she mumbled to Harriet as she brushed by her and headed for the street. 'Double-parked.'

It was a long slow drive out along Route Fifty, heading for Rancho Cordova. Twice she had to pull off the highway to wipe her eyes. 'I won't cry,' she told herself. Nobody seemed to notice, not even the Highway Patrolman bustling by her on his motor-cycle. Crying on the highway was *not* a crime, it appeared. A stop at the local shopping mall brought enough food for her to

hibernate for a few days. At one o'clock, when she let
herself into the old farm house, she was dead tired. Too
tired to carry in the groceries. She snatched out the milk
and the frozen orange juice, put them in the freezer, and
stumbled off up the stairs to bed. And that took care of
Monday.

Gloomy Tuesday. The skies were packed with
thunderheads, close enough to rattle the windows in the
old house. Philomena managed to climb out of bed and
paddle her way down to the kitchen. Coffee was the only
answer. Her head felt as if an elephant had stepped on it.
Her nose was stuffed up, cheeks red, and eyes rimmed
with black. 'Change the bed,' she reminded herself as her
hands fumbled for the makings. 'You've cried the pillow-
case to death.' As the pot perked she huddled herself up
into a little ball on the window seat, and stared out to
where the garden once had been. All gone. The garden,
the farm, the clump of willows that stood by the creek.
And even the creek itself, diverted to make room for
another high-rise.

Her conscience nagged her. 'Rape,' she had shouted
after him, and it hadn't been. Seduction—well, yes—but
there's no law against seducing your wife. And she had *so*
enjoyed it all. All except the last five minutes, when his
words had spoiled all his deeds. But it wasn't rape, and
her accusation had no foundation. 'I owe him an
apology,' she told herself as she reached for the
telephone. Her hand stopped before she picked up the
instrument. Talk to him? I'd sooner wrestle an alligator!
I don't *dare* to talk to him. Or face him, for that matter.
I'll—I'll write him a nice letter?

Thirty minutes and two cups of coffee later she was
still reaching for the telephone. I've *got* to call somebody,

she told herself as she dialled her sister Sally's number. There was no answer. She tried it again three times during the day, with the same result. Disgusted with the world, she suddenly remembered the groceries, still stacked in the car. Wrapped in her faded old green robe, she ventured out. It was raining as if someone had broken a dam somewhere in the sky overhead; coming down in sheets.

'Sunny California,' she muttered as she dodged back into the house, dressed, squeezed herself into her heavy rainwear, and went back for the groceries. And felt as stupid as she must have looked. While she was forcing herself into her sou'wester coat the thunderstorms had rolled on towards the mountains, and the sun was sparkling at her.

By Wednesday she felt well enough to eat a decent meal. Put it all behind you, she ordered. It's time for Practical Pill to get her feet on the ground and go about living. She had a place to live, no job, and not a devil of a lot of money in her bank account. The house—well, it belonged to all the girls, not just to herself. To sell it would require action by the Trust, a couple of bank officials whose names she had already forgotten. So the first order of things must be to get a new job. She settled down with copies of both Sacramento papers and began to scan the sits. vac.

A very hard job that, scanning the ads. The print was small, and behind it lurked Penn's face. Smiling, laughing, accusing, pursuing, loving Penn. His face swam in miniature behind the advertising, then grew and grew until it filled the page, and held her, bound her, until the tears came to blot it all out. When she dried her eyes, the cycle started again. She threw the paper down and dialled Sally. Still no answer.

There were still two sisters left. But Deborah had gone to Tahoe for a ski-ing vacation, and if Samantha were actually at home she was not the person with whom Phil could share a confidence. So she put the telephone and the papers away and threw herself into a fury of house-cleaning. Her mind steadied under the diversion. At four o'clock that afternoon the doorbell rang, and she found herself running down the stairs in eagerness, almost singing. He had finally come!

She threw back the lock and opened the door expectantly. And there, standing on the bottom step, so that his eyes were just at the level of hers, was Penn. She brushed away the tears and stared. Black eyes, focusing on her, sending out pulses of anger, massive anger.

'Mrs Wilderman, I believe,' he said, in a voice that sounded like a steel rasp at work. She backed slowly away from him as he came up the steps and into the hall. It was as if Penn's anger were a terrible wind, forcing her backwards step by step down the hall, until she ran into the back wall. *I need to make a decision,* she screamed at herself. *No you don't,* that inner voice assured her. *The decision was made for you, a long time ago.*

All of Phil's resolution and fierce independence disappeared in one crashing collapse. She abandoned dignity and pride. With tears streaming down her face she ran straight ahead and threw her arms around her husband's waist. 'Oh, God, Penn,' she groaned into his sweater. 'I need you.'

He stood rigidly still for a moment as she huddled herself against him. *He's going to refuse me, she thought in panic.* But she was mistaken. His arms came around her, pressing her even tighter into the safe nest. His lips brushed lightly against her hair. So lightly that she could barely feel it. 'It's all right, love,' he said. 'I'm here. Everything will be all right.'

And she knew it would be so.

It took more time for the tears to slow and all the time he held her close, crooning into her hair.

'You didn't forget,' she finally stammered. 'I thought you had forgotten me!'

'I've never forgotten anything about you, since the day we met,' he said, suddenly very solemn, very believable. 'Everything except what you looked like, Philomena. You've been a rascal, *young* lady.'

'Yes,' she admitted freely. 'I—I didn't know how to tell you, and——'

'No matter,' he laughed. 'If I fell in love with you blindly—how much easier it is to love what I can see. There's an old Roman poem that goes something like *How much stronger Love must be, sweeter the touch, the kiss, the mind, if Love be blind*. You're a beautiful woman, Mrs Wilderman. Come on. Blow.' He offered her a handkerchief that seemed half an acre in size, then tucked her under his arm. She squeezed up against him, unwilling to be an inch from her anchor.

'I'm sorry,' she offered tentatively.

'I'm sorry? Is that all I get from my run-away wife? I'm sorry?'

'I—I don't know what else to say.'

'If it's conceivable, after all the things I've done to you, Phil, for you to say *I love you*, that would be a good place to start. Can you forgive me?'

'I—I don't need to forgive you.' Happy for the first time in days, she almost giggled at his serious face looming over her. 'I love you. I'm pretty stupid. I didn't find it out until the day we were married, Penn, but—I love you.'

'That's enough for now,' he returned as he leaned over and kissed her gently. 'Let's go home, wife.'

'Whatever you say,' she said, and did not recognise the proportion of her surrender until they were at the front door. The telephone rang behind them in the living-room. She stopped, and used the momentary break to quell her panic.

'Leave it alone,' he grumbled, reaching out for her.

'I—I can't,' she stammered, stalling for time to regain control of her very scattered senses. 'I—I have this thing about telephones. If I don't answer it, I'll have bad luck all the rest of the day!'

'That's about as crazy an excuse as I've heard,' he chuckled. 'The telephone is your servant, not your master. You don't *have* to jump every time it rings at you.' He did a quick scan of her worried little face. 'Or maybe you do. Well, I'll give you two minutes to get back out here.'

'Or else?'

'Or else I'll come and get you, wife.' He added a small push in the middle of her back to get her moving. She ran the rest of the way.

'Phil? It's Sally here. I think you're in a lot of trouble. Phil? Are you there?'

'I'm here, dear. What trouble could I be in?'

'Well, we just got back from our trip to Los Angeles about three hours ago, and the telephone was ringing when we drove up to the house. Your husband, it was. Mad as a hatter. Wanted to know where the family home was. I gave him the address—Phil, if you're in trouble, you'd better get out of there quick. He means to get you.'

'You're too late,' Phil giggled nervously, not quite sure of the status of things. 'He's already got me.'

'What in the world is going on, Phil?'

'I—you wouldn't believe it if I told you, Sally. I—I think I've managed to get him just where he wants me. I can't talk now. He hates to be kept waiting. Call me here tomorrow. If I answer you'll know I'm in a *lot* of trouble. G'bye.'

She barely managed to get the instrument back in its cradle. Her feet were busy running before her hand was finished 'putting down'.

'Relax,' he said, catching her on the fly, like an expert outfielder. 'You've still got thirty seconds.'

'Oh,' she sighed, out of breath and courage at the same time.

'But there's no need to waste all that allotted time,' he continued smoothly, and proceeded to kiss her very thoroughly. Even more shaken than before, she leaned against his arm as he helped her out to the Cadillac. Frank held the door for them. It was not until they were enclosed in the moving cocoon, out on the highway, that she regained a little aplomb.

'You used more than thirty seconds,' she accused him, doing her best to glare. 'What if we were really in a hurry?'

'First, lady, you need to remember that the boss doesn't have to account for his time. Got it?'

'I—yes. I—I've got it.'

'Good. Secondly, Robbie and Harry will be back tomorrow morning on the nine o'clock flight.'

'But that's—that's hours away.' The spirit was willing to dare, but her shaky voice demonstrated her weakness.

'Yes, isn't it?' A broad grin spread across his face, and

a devilish look gleamed in those dark, dark eyes of his.
She shivered. Whatever it was he was planning was
bound to be—bound to be! She shifted uneasily in her
seat, clenched her hands together in her lap, and did her
best to admire the scenery.

They were back at the mansion before she could
account for the time. Penn helped her out of the car, and
before she could muster the scream that ought to have
followed, he swept her up in his arms and carried her up
the stairs to the door. 'Put the car away, Frank, and take
the rest of the day off,' he called over his shoulder.

Murder, she thought wildly? He's getting rid of all the
witnesses? He's going to kiss me to death? Phil's head
kept spinning as he kicked the front door closed behind
them and bustled her into the living-room. The couch
bounced as he dropped her there.

'Now then, Philomena.' He pulled one of the straight-
backed chairs over directly in front of her, reversed it,
and sat down with arms resting on its back, almost nose
to nose with her.

'Yes?' Calm, cool Philomena—well, almost. With
those pads on his eyes, and then his glasses, she had never
noticed how neat and precise his nose was. How—
Roman? It was irresistible. She leaned forward and
planted a kiss on its end.

'Now cut that out,' he growled. 'First, we have a great
deal of talking to do, you and I.'

'Dictatorial,' she muttered. 'Pompous. What you mean
is you're going to talk and I'm going to listen, right?'

'No, it's not right,' he sighed. 'So I'm a little pompous.
You're a whole lot impulsive. And neither one of us is
really going to change.'

'I—suppose so,' she returned apologetically. 'Mama

always said you can't marry a man, meaning to change him to what you want. What did you want to talk about?'

'You and me,' he said. 'Your mother was some smart cookie. How old were you when you became house-mother?'

'I—seventeen. I was old for my age, though.'

'Of course you were.' His hand ruffled through her loose hair. 'And you kept on being older than your age, didn't you? That was a mean trick you played on me.'

'I—I didn't,' she returned indignantly. 'It was all in your mind. I never said I—you decided right away that I was some old biddy—what Harry called me, an old broad!'

'But you knew what I was thinking, and you never set me straight. Why?'

'I—at first I thought it didn't matter. We wouldn't have met again, ever. Until you suddenly had to have a new wardrobe for your son. It's all your fault! How did I know Robbie needed clothes, for goodness' sake?'

'He didn't.' There—in the background. He's laughing at me, she thought. I can hear it. Her temper was climbing, rescuing her from being a shrinking violet. A blush flooded her cheeks.

'What do you mean?' she said very slowly, very firmly.

'I mean Robbie had a cupboard full of clothes that we had to get rid of. It took me two or three days to think up that excuse.'

'Excuse? You sent me off with that little—with that boy as an excuse!'

'I had to think of something to get us back together again,' he chuckled. 'You have no idea what you put me through, Philomena Wilderman. There I was with this crazy feeling, for some—old broad—that I couldn't even see. I *had* to find some excuse to keep you close by until I could get all those crazy feelings under control. Instead, I kept getting deeper and deeper in the mud. But that wasn't the height of my scheming. The wedding—that was my centrepiece. A real out-and-out scam, that almost backfired.'

'You—you—rascal!' she gasped. 'You—the wedding—it wasn't because you needed a wife for the court hearing?'

He got up and spun his chair out of the way, and sat down on the couch beside her. One arm went around her stiff shoulders, the other covered both her hands, twisting and straining in her lap. 'Oh, I needed a wife,' he whispered in her ear, 'but not just for the hearing.'

'But—but you said it was only temporary—that after the hearing and all—you said—you'd make it all worth my while. That's what you said!'

'Well, in for a dime, in for a dollar,' he chuckled. His hand had come off her shoulder, and was toying with her ear lobe. 'I somehow had the feeling that you wouldn't buy the package without an escape clause.' And then, much more seriously, 'Do you want to escape, Phil?'

'Me?' She was struggling between laughter and tears, and the laughter won out. She relaxed, and snuggled up against him. 'Not me. I never had it so good!'

About five minutes later, while she struggled to regain her breath, he tickled her chin. 'I love kissing,' he chuckled.

'Well, don't be too free with your favours,' she snapped. 'I don't share.'

'Hey now, love, I don't either. We were lucky, you and I.'

'Lucky?'

'Of course. Robbie was always a problem. There was no way our marriage could work if you hadn't won him around.'

'It wasn't all my doing,' she sighed. 'The poor mixed-up kid thought I looked like his real mother. That picture of your sister—it seemed to connect us all. It gave me a first advantage with Robbie. And it gave me my first bad opinion of you. I thought that Robbie might have been—your illegitimate child, or something. And it wasn't until we went to the court hearing that I found out you were really his uncle. You could have told me outright, you know.'

'Sure I could have,' he chuckled. 'And would have lost your interest completely. I knew the boy had your attention, and as long as you thought I was his father you were hanging in there. I had few enough strings on you to afford to let one go. But you're right in one aspect. The painting did tie us together. When I came home Monday without the pads on my eyes I just couldn't wait to find you, to see what you looked like. And what did I see? My sister Robin standing in the door. I thought I had lost my wits, or something, so I rushed up the stairs to look at her portrait, and by the time I came down again you were gone. I thought—well, I was high—on excitement, not alcohol—on Sunday night. And when you yelled rape at me and then ran away, I figured I had really blown the works.'

'It wasn't rape,' she sighed, and moved as close as she could. 'I knew it at the time, and I know it now. It was just that—well, afterwards—you seemed to be so disgusted with it all that I thought—I just wanted to hurt you back, and that's why—I'm sorry, Penn. It wasn't rape. I'm your wife, you were very gentle, and I did enjoy it so much. I—I never thought I could—I just didn't know about that sort of wonderful excitement.'

He heaved a sigh of relief after the explanation. 'I thought I really had done us in,' he told her. 'I thought I deserved to be miserable—that I ought to let you go.'

'I'm glad you didn't.'

'Well, that was only for a couple of minutes that I had that crazy idea,' he laughed. 'And then I called the office, and lo and behold, someone had erased all of Philomena Peabody's records. Who could have done that?'

'Who indeed?' she murmured in a very quiet voice. There were some interesting patterns in the wallpaper. She studied them carefully. Anything rather than look into those eyes.

'And then your sister—I had her telephone number, but nobody answered. Do you realise that I had two secretaries at the office do nothing for three days but dial your sister's telephone every fifteen minutes, day and night?'

'It must have cost you a fortune in overtime.'

'Don't be sarcastic,' he laughed. 'I'll get it all back. I'm a persistent guy.'

The wallpaper lost its interest. She turned around to face him, treasuring his face between her two soft hands. 'I'm very glad for that,' she confessed. 'I'm a very stubborn woman. I might have held off from calling you for—oh—at least another week. Maybe two.'

Confession is good for the soul, she told herself a few minutes later. My, doesn't he taste good! But there's something going on around here that I can't quite figure out. He's up to something! She shivered deliciously, in anticipation.

He raised his hand to check his wristwatch. 'Three

o'clock,' he announced. 'And Robbie will be back tomorrow. I should have arranged for the kid to spend *two* weeks fishing.'

'Why—that's unkind, Penn. That's my son you're talking about.'

'So it is. Well, I think you'd better run up to your room and have a nap, Phil.'

'Nap? I'm not tired. I'm so excited I couldn't sleep. I—why?'

'I'm glad you're not tired,' he chuckled. 'Scoot upstairs.'

She went, but reluctantly, dragging her feet, stopping to smile at his sister's picture, winking an eye at the Pirate King. By the time she wandered into her room he was right behind her, with two glasses in his hand. 'Champagne,' he said. 'Let's drink a toast to the time when the pompous overcome the impulsive.'

'Or vice versa,' she giggled, gulping the contents at one swallow. 'Oops, I forgot.' She hiccupped. 'What are you doing?'

'How does this damn thing come off?'

'There's a zipper in the back,' she whispered in a very tiny voice. The glass slipped out of her hand and fell, but did not break. Her blouse slipped off her shoulders. His warm breath on her skin started her quivering. He needed no other invitation.

An hour later, satiated, she lay stretched out flat on her back, all her limbs askew, like some wanton Eve. He lay on his side, facing her. Perspiration stood on his forehead. She used a finger to trace letters in it, then dried it off with her loose hair.

'What are you writing on me?' he asked.

'A message,' she responded. "Penn Wilderman Belongs To Me." I intend to have one made for each of your cars, and two to go in your office.'

'Are you really? Pretty possessive, aren't you, Mrs Wilderman.'

'I—yes,' she stated very firmly. Practical Pill was back in action. Everything seemed under control. Except—it had been a wild hour, but how could she know if it had been as wild for him as it had been for her?

'Penn?'

'Yes. I'm still here.' His hand was tracing circles in her hair.

'Penn, that wasn't too shabby for—for an old broad, was it?'

'For a beginner I'd rate that as a ten plus,' he laughed. 'Were you worried? I never would have thought that you would catch on so quickly. And that's enough with the *old broad* business.'

'I—well. I wanted to talk seriously—stop that!' His index finger was probing at the spot just under her ribcage—the only spot on her entire body that was ticklish. She squealed as she wriggled away from him and seized the punishing digit. 'Don't do that,' she giggled. 'I hate being tickled.' Her hand pulled his finger up to her mouth. She snapped her sharp little teeth at it without touching, and then kissed it gently.

'Hey, for a minute there——' He rolled over on his stomach, half on top of her.

'That's just to remind you that I don't put up with any foolishness,' she giggled.

'Even from your husband?'

'Especially from my husband. I wanted to talk seriously about something.'

'Now? Here? Boy, you can always tell who the

amateurs are, can't you.'

'Amateurs? I thought I had just become a professional. Stop that!' Two tickling fingers this time, one on either side. She snatched them both up and held them. Talk fast, you fool, she told herself. Talk fast.

'It's about Robbie.'

'Oh.' His fingers stopped wriggling. 'Even in our bridal bed? *What* about Robbie?'

'It's just that—I think it's a bad mistake, having an only child in the family, and I'm not really getting any younger, so if we intend to do something about it we'll have to be fairly quick, and—what are you doing?' A *frisson* of alarm in her voice, as he rolled over again, on top of her, and began that tickling assault.

She did her best to squirm away, but his weight pinned her in place like a butterfly in a showcase. 'What are you doing?' Barely forced out, this time, because of the wild giggling she could not suppress. He stopped.

'What am I doing?' That Voice of Doom tone of his, suddenly broken off in the deep bass of his own laughter. 'You presented me a problem. Robbie needs a little sister. These things don't come easily. I may have to work on it for some time to come.' Those hands again, not poking, not tickling, moving slowly up to the under-curve of her breasts.

'You silly man,' she said in a soft, love-filled voice. The fingers moved on and his lips came down on her. Everything else was lost as her world dissolved in flames.

Six exciting series for you every month... from Harlequin

Harlequin Romance
The series that started it all

Tender, captivating and heartwarming...
love stories that sweep you off to faraway places
and delight you with the magic of love.

◆

Harlequin Presents
Powerful contemporary love stories...as individual as the women who read them

The No. 1 romance series...
exciting love stories for you, the woman of today...
a rare blend of passion and dramatic realism.

◆

Harlequin Superromance®
It's more than romance...
it's Harlequin Superromance

A sophisticated, contemporary romance-fiction
series, providing you with a longer,
more involving read...a richer mix of complex plots,
realism and adventure.

Harlequin
American Romance™
Harlequin celebrates the
American woman...

...by offering you romance stories written
about American women, by American women
for American women. This series offers you
contemporary romances uniquely North American
in flavor and appeal.

◆

Harlequin Temptation™
Passionate stories for
today's woman

An exciting series of sensual, mature stories of
love...dilemmas, choices, resolutions...
all contemporary issues dealt with in a true-to-life
fashion by some of your favorite authors.

◆

Harlequin Intrigue
Because romance can be quite
an adventure

Harlequin Intrigue, an innovative series that
blends the romance you expect...
with the unexpected. Each story has an added
element of intrigue that provides a new twist to
the Harlequin tradition of romance excellence.

Harlequin Books·

PROD-A-2

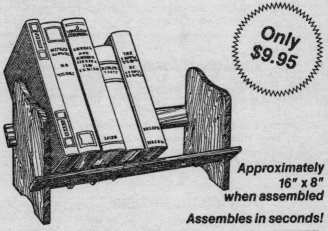